Tiny Treasures

THE EAST MIDLANDS & THE EAST

First published in Great Britain in 2010 by
Young Writers, Remus House, Coltsfoot Drive,
Peterborough, PE2 9JX
Tel (01733) 890066 Fax (01733) 313524
Website: www.youngwriters.co.uk

Disclaimer
Young Writers has maintained every effort
to publish stories that will not cause offence.
Any stories, events or activities relating to individuals
should be read as fictional pieces and not construed
as real-life character portrayal.

Book designed by Spencer Hart & Tim Christian

Foreword

Since Young Writers was established in 1990, our aim has been to promote and encourage written creativity amongst children and young adults. By giving aspiring young authors the chance to be published, Young Writers effectively nurtures the creative talents of the next generation, allowing their confidence and writing ability to grow.

With our latest fun competition, *The Adventure Starts Here ...*, primary school children nationwide were given the tricky challenge of writing a story with a beginning, middle and an end in just fifty words.

The diverse and imaginative range of entries made the selection process a difficult but enjoyable task with stories chosen on the basis of style, expression, flair and technical skill. A fascinating glimpse into the imaginations of the future, we hope you will agree that this entertaining collection is one that will amuse and inspire the whole family.

To Nana and
Grandad,
Hope you like it.

From Sam

XXX

Contents

Frisby CE Primary School, Melton Mowbray

The Downs CE Primary School, Deal

Whitehills Primary School, Northampton

Woodlands School, Brentwood

The Mini Sagas

I Didn't Know!

Today was the worst day ever! I walked through a door. Guess what! I went through and entered my best friend's body! I felt spiteful and evil. Keep it a secret but I punched her. Now I know how she feels.
Later that day I told her I was sorry!

Amelia Bailey (11)
Brownlow School, Melton Mowbray

The Note

I sat by the door and the bell rang, *Ding dong*. The door creaked as I opened it to see outside. There was a note on the doorstep: 'Meet me at the corner of the street at 12pm.'
I trudged to the corner of the street in silence …

Daniel Smith (11)
Brownlow School, Melton Mowbray

Incy Spider All Over Again

Incy Wincy Spider slid down the gutter pipe,
the water soon became frozen. He was stuck
for good! The sun didn't come out for days.
Eventually Incy ran out of food, however he drank
the ice! Finally the sun shone, defrosting the ice.
Incy swam down the pipe - free again!

Joe Tarris (11)
Brownlow School, Melton Mowbray

Boat Trail

The bright sun was beaming on the freezing cold sea, when one day a family was going on a boat trip in Spain. They were half way out in the sea when the boat started to sink. Water started to pour into the boat and everyone got worried (Argh!) Dead!

Conor Robson (10)
Brownlow School, Melton Mowbray

4

The Dungeon

The wind danced in and out of the dungeon. Kelly sat alone. She felt like the walls were closing in on her. The chains clanged against the wall. The room fell silent. She heard something moving. It sounded ghost-like. Spooky. And then, 'Argh!'

Georgia Clater (10)
Brownlow School, Melton Mowbray

5

Cloe's Nightmare

'Cloe you may go now!' After a boring day at school I was glad to go home. Nobody was in! 'Hello!' I shouted. 'Is anyone here?' Suddenly the door flung open. It was Paige. However something strange had happened to her. She was flying. I screamed. She was playing.

Jade Willatt (11)

Brownlow School, Melton Mowbray

6

Incy Wincy Spider

Incy Wincy Spider climbed up the castle wall, then
came the snow that froze the spider stiff. Next
came the rain which froze him even more. Finally
came the sun that melted the ice away. Incy
climbed again. However when he got to the top,
he was shell-shocked.

Benjamin LeCoyte (10)
Brownlow School, Melton Mowbray

The Legend Of The Towers

One night the Earl was riding home in his horse and carriage when a strange figure appeared in the road. The Earl demanded his driver to carry on. The old woman didn't like that. The old woman put a curse on the Earl. That night the Earl very strangely died.

Aaron Starkey (11)
Brownlow School, Melton Mowbray

The Reunion: Tara And Tulala

Tara exited the plane wearing a dress. As soon
she got off she felt the hot Majorcan air hit her.
Then she saw the face, the flaming red hair of
Tulala. The spitefulness seemed to have died since
the last visit. Last time, well Tara was injured
badly - not good!

Rosella Hazeldine (10)
Brownlow School, Melton Mowbray

Friday's The Bad Day

It was a Friday morning, Miss Storm gave out
invitations to a party. When the children got
home they showed the invitation to their parents
and they let them go. They all arrived at the party
and were eaten by the hungry vampires. What
were their parents gong to say?

Alfie Farmer (10)
Brownlow School, Melton Mowbray

A Halloween Surprise

As Maisie walked down her path she saw
something in her window. Suddenly a bang and
a scream came from her house. Running in to
see what was happening, she saw blood-dripping
vampires and ghosts. She turned to a woman who
said, 'Happy Halloween, hope I didn't scare you!'

Molly Irish (11)
Brownlow School, Melton Mowbray

The Vampire And The Wolf

One dark day a scruffy werewolf which was black
and grey went up to a crumbling house where
a vampire lived. The vampire was black with a
red cape. They went to the freaky dark park,
however it was not freaky to them. It matched
their image - dark, freaky, horrid!

Jake Mogg (10)
Brownlow School, Melton Mowbray

The Ghostly Mansion

The man walked into the mansion. Suddenly a one-armed alien ran towards the man. The man ran into the kitchen. Then a see-through ghost appeared. Then there appeared a hairy monster with massive jaws. Then the huge-jawed monster opened his mouth and quickly ate the man. Tasty!

Kai Meeks (10)
Brownlow School, Melton Mowbray

Kelly The Nelly

Once there was a girl called Kelly. Everyone knew
her in the town of Cuntly, she was big and bold.
She thought she knew everything but she didn't.
But now everyone likes her because she ditched
the stupid 'fella' character and horrible character.
Now she has loads of friends!

Lucy Baxter (10)
Brownlow School, Melton Mowbray

The Dragon

Firstly Fred the dragon scampered to his wooden
house, had a cup of tea, then went to find some
dinner. He found, killed and ate a fish. Eventually
he went back to his grand house, read a book
called 'Bears' then sat down, got comfortable and
fell asleep in chair.

Jack Knight (11)
Brownlow School, Melton Mowbray

The Werewolf Unmasked

The evil vampire darted across the empty field. When he reached the deserted house the door burst open. 'Argh!' he yelled. Staring him in the eyes was a massive werewolf. The wolf barked and slowly started wrenching his face off. 'Noo!' the vampire screamed. It was just Jasper, his brother.

Emily Hubbard (11)
Brownlow School, Melton Mowbray

The Werewolf Diaries

On a stormy night, Jacob Black suddenly turned into a werewolf, racing toward Bella Swan, who quickly ran out of the way. Bella ran to her house and laid down on the sofa. She hoped that it wasn't real. She woke up startled. It was definitely true. He was there …

Gemma Chapman (10)
Brownlow School, Melton Mowbray

17

Safe!

Britney saw it. As she strolled through the sludgy field to meet her grandma she saw a twisted hunched-back figure. It turned towards her. She started to run. It followed her. She hid behind a damp, mossy tree … Something wrinkly grabbed her … It was her grandma. She was safe.

Libby Ellis (11)
Brownlow School, Melton Mowbray

Nelly Kelly

Nelly Kelly jumped on the wall. Nelly Kelly ran to the mall. All the shopkeepers and the security guards had to take Nelly to the hospital, only a couple of yards. As they got there it was closed, so poor old Nelly slowly walked home and had a doze!

Georgia Goodbourne (11)
Brownlow School, Melton Mowbray

The Vampire Diaries

Edward sat there on his porch, all alone, waiting for human blood. There she was, walking down L'Push. He sneaked up behind her and ... bit her. He injected venom into her heart. She was a vampire. She was violent. Oh no, I lay there looking at her. Was it real?

Lauren Rudd (10)
Brownlow School, Melton Mowbray

The Vampire Attack

As the vampire showed his razor-sharp fangs,
Annie knew this was the end. The werewolf was
dead, and now she would be. Closing her eyes,
Annie waited for death to come. Suddenly pain
shot through her, causing her to cry out. Slowly
she sank into the blissfulness of death.

Maddie Price (11)
Brownlow School, Melton Mowbray

21

From Behind The Computer

With a bang the computer died. I couldn't bring it back to life. Suddenly a small green slimy creature walked from behind the computer. It walked to my hand, unfortunately, 'Ouch!' it bit me. I was going bright purple. Just then I felt really light, I was in Heaven finally.

Amy Cornforth (10)
Brownlow School, Melton Mowbray

The Dino Tree

I was skateboarding down the street, dreaming about dinosaurs, when *wham!* I hit a giant tree, however when I looked up it had a mouth. I fainted and when I woke up it was just a boring old tree. I rode home as quickly as I could over the road.

Ashley Parker (11)
Brownlow School, Melton Mowbray

Prowling Wolf

Prowling through the woods he sees a vampawolf sucking on a queen's juicy but raw neck. The thing is he likes royal blood. Previously there have been reports that the vampawolf eats girls walking home from school. Quickly the wolf turns, the vampawolf is advancing, fangs ready for the kill …

Jayde McCallum (11)
Brownlow School, Melton Mowbray

Haunted Castle

One mysterious morning I woke up with some of my friends - Jake, Kai, Kieren and Jacob. We went to the mysterious haunted castle. We all knocked on the door, it was so spooky, we jumped out of our skins. So we ran quickly home before we died and told Mum.

Brandon Sharpe (10)
Brownlow School, Melton Mowbray

Untitled

There was an old corner house. Molly and Libby crept in, suddenly ghostly things were flying around them. Blood marks were smeared over the dirty, crumbling walls. A grumpy, wizened old man appeared, shouting, 'Get out of my house!' Quickly Molly and Libby ran away from the spooky house forever.

Hannah Lee (10)

Brownlow School, Melton Mowbray

Battle Of The Dragon

Entering the dank cellar, a freezing wind spiralled
towards me. I noticed the dragons had begun.
They twisted, slashed and turned as Death fought.
Sneakily the astounding white dragon feinted
a move and ripped Death itself to shreds. The
power of light has defeated the deathly terrible
darkness once again …

Daniel Bennett (10)
Brownlow School, Melton Mowbray

The Scary Light

Annabell slowly walked in, her heart beating fast as she saw the light flickering on and off. She got very scared. She turned around very slowly with her eyes shut. She saw Thomas with the light switch. She screamed, 'It was you!' She was very, very cross and unhappy.

Kaitlin Mann (10)

Brownlow School, Melton Mowbray

The Vampire Diaries

Edward sat all alone on his sofa waiting for some human blood, seeing a human approaching Oxford Street. Then he quickly crept up behind him and snapped at the neck. Then he injected venom into the heart and suddenly the human rose and he was a tall, dark, fearsome vampire.

Kieren Skinner (11)

Brownlow School, Melton Mowbray

Blood Suckers

Joseph had finally realised what he had got himself into. He was cured by the blood-dripping pixie queen. Yet how could he escape before being devoured into her stomach? Still he had to find a way out. Suddenly she struck Joseph with one of her fangs, he became evil.

Mollie Wheatley (11)
Brownlow School, Melton Mowbray

The Apocalpyse Has Begun

'Rider!' Mr Grey shouted. Alex looked up at the
hard equation on the board.
'X equals seven and Y equals nine.' He replied.
'Thank you,' Mr Grey said. When he was fully
prepared Alex thought about the snakehead's
15,000 hawk tactical nukes very carefully aimed at
the other large continents ...

David Stockdale (11)
Brownlow School, Melton Mowbray

The Mysterious Bang

John stared at the freshly painted door as the mysterious bang from the other side frightened him stiff. He knew that the only person on that side was his teacher, Mr Collins. John had only gone to the toilet and yet his teacher was unstapling his best work. 'Oh no!'

Luke Parkin (11)
Brownlow School, Melton Mowbray

Werewolf Surprise

Maddie watched her step as she walked into the
forest. The feeling was strange. Suddenly she
heard a rustle behind her. She very slowly turned
around. Her friend became a horrifying werewolf.
Now there was a secret, her friend was a killer!
She fell to the ground …

Elizabeth Hunt (11)

Brownlow School, Melton Mowbray

The Haunted House

On a dark, miserable day in a wood, a little boy
called Tom cycled towards a black spooky house.
He was meant to meet his friend there, however
after a while he still wasn't there. The boy went
into the house and walked towards the stairs.
Suddenly 'Surprise!' shouted Luke.

Tyler Simmonds (11)
Brownlow School, Melton Mowbray

Death

The light flickered on and off, the ghost was coming, the dread was present. I could feel death, the wind of his breath, the chill of his hands. I was going to die. By now I was even feeling his heartbeat, he was slowly but surely trying to kill me.

Lewis Hurrell (10)

Brownlow School, Melton Mowbray

The Clown

I was on my way home. I ran. What should I do? I looked back at him; he looked like an evil clown. I fell, he caught me. I got away. When I got home he got in. 'Mum? Dad?' I shouted. He killed me.

Jack Anderson (11)
Brownlow School, Melton Mowbray

A Day In The Life Of ...

Today was the strangest day of my life! I was just sitting quietly watching TV, when all of a sudden a door popped into the room. It was extraordinary. Before I knew it I was in my best friend's body! I never knew what it was like to be her.

Lily Goddard (10)
Brownlow School, Melton Mowbray

The Deadly Knock

Knock, knock, knock! 'Who is it?'
'Your worst nightmare.'
Sharon didn't know who or what was at the door.
Two army men fell in. Their faces mauled to the
bone. In distress Sharon slammed the door …

Joseph Thorn (11)
Brownlow School, Melton Mowbray

Easter Time

There was a girl called Laura, it was Easter evening, she was very excited. She sprinted to bed and couldn't get to sleep. Eventually she nodded off. She work up in the morning, ran downstairs, found there were no treats! She sat down and sobbed. She felt something. Treats!

Eleanor Lapworth (8)
Desford Community Primary School, Desford

Bonfire Night

It was Bonfire Night. Lauren was reading in bed.
A moment later - *bang!* She heard something. She
went to investigate. She opened the back door
and bravely slipped out. She saw two people, she
got scared. Then they said to Lauren, 'Come join
in.' It was her mum and dad.

Holly Turner (7)
Desford Community Primary School, Desford

Under The Sea

Dr Fisher was driving the hawk sub when he saw a glowing object. 'What's this?' he said to himself. Suddenly a spear landed next to him and a giant turtle charged towards the sub. Dr Fisher jumped in and fired a missile. But the turtle warrior had disappeared.

Rory Cunningham (9)
Desford Community Primary School, Desford

41

The Nightmare On Elm Street

One night, in a street called Elm Street, a girl called Lois was having a terrible nightmare about a man called Freddy Crobger. He had pins all over, he also had a glove with knives for fingers. Just then she woke up and the man was still there …

Tyler Chesterton (9)
Desford Community Primary School, Desford

The Big Dream

Bang! What happened? Where were we? We were on a remote island, a remote island with my brother! He looked at the trees, horrific faces stared right into us. We walked towards the trees and into the creepy, eerie forest. I awoke - it was all a dream.

Katie Peake (8)
Desford Community Primary School, Desford

The Creepy Noise

Ben, Adam and Daisy entered the room. They heard a strange noise. It was dark, they couldn't find the light switch. It was coming closer and closer. They tried to find the phone. The noise turned on the light and it was Mum and Dad cooking the dinner!

Rebecca Day (8)
Desford Community Primary School, Desford

The Scare Amy Had At Night

Amy was in bed fast asleep but just then she heard a noise that made her wake up. In her room there was a knight with silver armour and the knight said, 'I'm coming to get you!' Just then he lifted his helmet and it was Tom!

Olivia Feltus (8)
Desford Community Primary School, Desford

45

The Fantastic Birthday Of Fun!

Billy was back from tennis club. When he got back Mum said she was there. Suddenly the kitchen door flew open. His friends and family shouted, 'Happy birthday!' Suddenly a creak came from upstairs. Everyone screamed but the dog came prancing down the stairs like he hadn't done anything!

Mia Lee (8)

Desford Community Primary School, Desford

Trick Or Treat?

Katie and Matt were playing and suddenly everything went black, they were very scared. Just then two white images appeared. The lights flickered and they saw two googly eyes! They followed them and turned the lights on and Mum and Dad said, 'Trick or treat?'

Reneè Hope (9)
Desford Community Primary School, Desford

Creepy Forest

Max and Polly go on a picnic, they get lost. They see a forest and as soon as they walk in a sign pops up from nowhere. The sign says: *Enter If You Dare. Find A Unicorn That Is Lost In Time.* They find the unicorn and save it!

Jacob Sanderon (9)
Desford Community Primary School, Desford

The Nightmare

One night a girl woke up from a terrible nightmare. So she went to the bathroom to get a drink. As she was walking back she heard heavy breathing. She got in bed … and no one ever saw the girl again.

Ryan Lander (9)
Desford Community Primary School, Desford

Underground

One night in England, underground in a dark room, two good robbers nicked the amazing treasure chest. Mo, Jacob and Bart stopped them by getting there first and hiding behind the gold treasure chest. They set up an evil trap. They waited with loaded guns ...

Aidan Laws (7)

Desford Community Primary School, Desford

The Plan

One morning, in Egypt, a man called Tommy
woke up - he didn't have a home. He was thinking
of a plan to steal some gold from a tomb. He
bought an electric snake and led it into the tomb.
He stole the gold and lived a life of guilt.

Prianka Lakhani (9)
Desford Community Primary School, Desford

Secret Money

One day there lived a man called Tump. He was a strange man. He decided to win medals. He had lots of money. He moved to a posh house, next to it was a cottage where he kept his money. A girl pretended to be a mummy, she got arrested!

Georgia Tucker (8)
Desford Community Primary School, Desford

Tomb Heroes

It was 5am in the valley. 'Nearly there,' puffed
Martine. She got down the enormous stairs to
Tutankhamun's tomb. 'Ben?' Martine pondered as
she opened the stone door.
'Help!'
'Ben? It's you!'
'Yeah!'
I'm coming! Where are you?'
'In the coffin!'
Martine opened it. *Creak!* 'Run!' They got home!

Elisha Chauhan (9)
Desford Community Primary School, Desford

Egypt

One day in the desert there was a pyramid. An explorer went in the pyramid for treasure. He went down 1000 steps to the treasure, but a mummy was guarding it with a scorpion. The explorer went in the garden and hid. The man looked, took photos then left forever.

Grace Sprules (8)
Desford Community Primary School, Desford

The Shock

Lily was wandering up the road when she heard
a blood-curdling scream. She sprinted up the
road to her chalet in ancient Egypt. Lily had a long
blue dress and long curly hair. She reached the
chalet and her mum was shaking. She had seen
Tutankhamun wrapped in bandages!

Tess Grewcock (9)
Desford Community Primary School, Desford

Untitled

Once there was a man who kept mummy
stuff. On Bamby Road lived Dorothy. Her mum
ordered, 'Take some chocolate to the man.' She
fell on the way and turned into a mummy! She
heard an ice cream van. She jumped out and she
got arrested!

Jessica Hill (9)
Desford Community Primary School, Desford

Tomb

One day in Egypt there were two robbers named Bill and Will. They were trying to steal Tutankhamun's coffin. They tried to get into the pyramid but it was that strong stone! They could not get into it so they tried a different side. They could not get in!

Georgina Tebbutt (9)
Desford Community Primary School, Desford

The Mummy Escape

One boiling day in Egypt there was a man called Eric. He heard a clanking noise in an old disgusting tomb, so he broke in to see what was happening. He saw nothing. He waited a couple of minutes. A mummy killed him. That was the end of Eric!

Lauren Hull (8)

Desford Community Primary School, Desford

The Escaping Mummy

One day three people went to Egypt. One of the
men whispered, 'There's a tomb over there.'
The men broke into the tomb and they opened
the mummy case. A mummy came to life. The
mummy chased them, but the Egyptian got eaten
by the mummy.

Libby Finch (8)
Desford Community Primary School, Desford

A Pharaoh's Tomb

Once there was a pharaoh called Tutankhamun who died and then was mummified alive. Two years later he was found by an Egyptian child, but the Egyptian child then was cursed. 70,000 years later he was found by a chubby archaeologist but the poor man was eaten!

Caleb Hough (8)

Desford Community Primary School, Desford

Near An Erupting Volcano

Once upon a time a volcano erupted and the country shook. Everyone ran to a tree and climbed it. When this happened, some other people instead of running to a tree and climbing it, they held their breaths underwater. The lava stopped. They lived happily ever after.

James Green (7)
Desford Community Primary School, Desford

Untitled

I was walking home from my archaeologist training at dawn. Suddenly I fell through a dark hole and found myself in an Egyptian tomb. Then I saw a shiny coffin, but it was open wide. Something grabbed me - it was an Egyptian skeleton.

Harrison Newball-Underwood (8)

Desford Community Primary School, Desford

Meaneus And The Thinotor

Once there was a horrid man named Meaneus.
Meaneus also had a green monobrow! He went
to kill a creature called the Thinotor. He crossed
deserts, mountains and seas. When he arrived at
the cave, he heard a growl. He went in and slayed
the horrible Thinotor.

Aaron Chan (9)
Desford Community Primary School, Desford

The Forest

One day Ben and Katie were taking a walk down the lake. Ben asked Katie if he could go in the forest. Katie said, 'No, it is too dangerous for you to go in there.'
A few minutes later Ben pretended that he had fallen over …

Cole Baker (8)
Desford Community Primary School, Desford

The Spooky House

Once upon a time there was a boy called Max.
He was about to go into his room when he heard
ghosts. In fact it was Mum and Dad hoovering.
Then they were going to do a lot of dusting and
moving stuff. 'Ha-ha!' said Mum.

Adam Tsang (7)
Desford Community Primary School, Desford

Gandow's Tomb

In 2010, on Friday 26th March, in Egypt, Indiana
was trying to nick the treasure. He took a fellow
called Max. Max took the treasure because
Indiana had been killed by Gandow. He buried
Indy in his garden.

Brandon Pye (8)
Desford Community Primary School, Desford

The Pharaoh's Tomb

I was walking in the desert one day and suddenly
I slipped through a hole and I was in a place with
spiders and scorpions. In the centre of the room
was a coffin. I stepped forward and suddenly a
hand shot at me for a minute …

Valerian Beaujot (8)
Desford Community Primary School, Desford

Creak!

Lucy's unbrushed brown curly hair surrounded
her pale white face. Suddenly her ears pricked
up. She heard something coming from behind the
door. Then the creak got louder. She clutched the
handle and turned it. Outside was Martha. The
door had stuck, and she couldn't enter.

Charlotte Prime (10)

Desford Community Primary School, Desford

A Night At Granny's House

Lying in the dark room the sound of footsteps
met my ears. I turned but the dust got in my eyes.
I cried as two mysterious green eyes met mine.
I opened the door. The cat wrapped around my
legs and ran out of the room.

Georgia Turner (9)
Desford Community Primary School, Desford

The Mystery Noise

As Jemima's hair swung in the wind her friends
and English teacher swiftly followed her into the
cave of doom! As they sat down an eerie noise
crept through the cave. Everyone screamed and
ran out. What could that noise have been … ? It
was just the wind!

Rebecca Horne (10)

Desford Community Primary School, Desford

Haunted Fun

I was being chased by a gang of zombies through a haunted house. The gang was then joined by a werewolf. They were catching me up, but then I took a left turn into a dark corner. I lost them in there …
I love going to Steven's birthday parties.

Liam Fraser (10)
Desford Community Primary School, Desford

The Bedroom

Tom lay silent. He knew he wasn't alone. He could hear footsteps walking up the stairs. Tom looked at his door. He could see a headless man. He closed his eyes and hid. Tom decided to turn on the light. It was only his dressing gown!

Rose Sanderson (11)

Desford Community Primary School, Desford

The Scared Face

Kimberley was the sneakiest girl in town. She had just pulled a marvellous prank on her cousins and was on her way to the place where they lived. When she arrived, she opened the door. A witch's face came out. Kimberley jumped so high, she could see her cousins giggling.

Charley Colman (10)
Desford Community Primary School, Desford

The Day Cedric Went Up The Hill!

Cedric was racing up the hill with his long shaggy hair. On the hill there was a well where Cedric was fetching a bottle of water for his mother. He got to the top where the well was, it was slippery! He slipped, fell down the hill, thankfully he survived!

Jemima Garrett (9)
Desford Community Primary School, Desford

Sedrick's Accident

'Hello I'm Sedrick,' said Amelia flicking her golden hair. Amelia was refusing to eat the banana named Sedrick. 'Blah, blah, blah' murmured Jemima, staring through her glasses. Meanwhile Amelia was too busy listening to Jemima when she accidentally ate Sedrick! 'Oh no, you ate Sedrick,' screamed Jemima. We started crying.

Amelia Tolley (10)
Desford Community Primary School, Desford

75

Holiday

Juliette was stroking her long, blonde hair. She was lounging in a five-star hotel. The silver taps gleamed. The greasy-haired waiter brought her lemonade. Oddly she could hear rumbling noises and people talking. Suddenly Juliette found herself on a crowded street, staring at a Thompson's holiday billboard.

Evie Hiett Minto (9)

Desford Community Primary School, Desford

Surprise Party

Pat walked up to the old farmhouse. Nobody was there. He knocked on the rotting door. *Creak!* It slowly creaked open. Then suddenly a dog ran past and made Pat jump as high as an elephant! He walked in the farmhouse.
'Surprise!' they said. 'Happy birthday Pat.'

Kerry Fraser (10)
Desford Community Primary School, Desford

Sweet Tooth

Old Granny was very fit. She was so fit that she
had grown many wrinkles over her body. She was
in an old Victorian hotel, but she kept hearing
things that weren't normal. 'Who is talking?'
She then realised that the muffins were sending
her messages. 'Eat me.'
She smiled.

Kieran Evans-Hughes (11)
Desford Community Primary School, Desford

Three Little Kittens

The three little kittens were going to get some
meat, milk and biscuits. Then the big bad dog
came along and frightened the kittens away.
The big bad dog ate the kittens' meat, milk and
biscuits. But the kittens came back and hissed.
The big bad dog ran away fast.

Shania Fradsham (9)
Desford Community Primary School, Desford

The Ride Of Fear!

As soon as I entered the roller coaster ride I could feel fear down my body. I stepped on. *Crash. Swish.* 'I can hear water. Oh no! I can't get off!' *Creak.* It gradually started to move. 'I wish I hadn't come on this.' Faster and faster. 'Whee- what fun!'

William Newball-Underwood (9)
Desford Community Primary School, Desford

The Pebble

There I stood on the hillside, clutching a beautiful
pebble. Suddenly a flash of light shot past me. My
whole body shook with fear. I felt the pebble's
warmth. Dazzled by what I saw, I fell to my
knees. My whole body now swimming in precious
jewels. What treasure!

Katie Hardy (10)
Desford Community Primary School, Desford

The Apple And The Boy

One sunny day a boy picked up an apple and put it in his pocket. He jumped up and started flying! He rose higher and higher. He felt like a bird. He saw tiny fields below him, he swooped and looped, and the apple fell out. He fell down.
Thump!

Alice Holder (10)
Desford Community Primary School, Desford

Fire

A boy, Jim, walked around a town when he saw
a toy on the floor. He picked it up. He started to
feel hot. Suddenly he was on fire! 'I'm on fire!'
So he flew around. 'Finally I've had enough.' He
dropped the car. That was the end of him.

James Bacon (10)
Desford Community Primary School, Desford

The Old Silly Lady

Speeding through the shop door I had lost total control of my wheelchair, screaming at people to move out of the way. The looks they were giving me were so unkind. I swung to the right, there it stood, an enormous tower of 1kg boxes of delicious crunchy nut cereals …

Britney Burrows (11)
Desford Community Primary School, Desford

War

Frightened, I froze to the spot. In front of me
stood a machine as big as a skyscraper. *Bang!*
Noise surrounded me everywhere. Then
deafness hit me. People running, faces full of fear.
I could see their pain yet I could hear no sound.
Was this what war is about?

Kyle Blyth (9)
Desford Community Primary School, Desford

Victorian Mine Fright

As I stepped into the mine I felt scared and nervous. The door slammed behind me and left me in the dark. Fear was running down my back. What was that? Water! I needed to get out. I ran as fast as my little legs could carry me. Light! Safety!

Ellen Sanderson (10)
Desford Community Primary School, Desford

Help

Suddenly a blurry sensation took over Tom.
A wood was forming around him. *Crash!* An
emerald-green dragon landed beside him. He
showed his teeth. Each one was as sharp as a
pitchfork. Bats encircled him. A familiar voice got
to his ear. 'School time.'

Adele Ketley (9)
Frisby CE Primary School, Melton Mowbray

Sharks!

Splash! Jessica played in the sea while her parents watched. Suddenly she'd gone! They searched everywhere but could only see two sharp shark fins. Quickly Dad jumped into the icy water. Jessica's head popped up between the shark fins. 'Dad,' come and swim between these pointy rocks,' Jessica said happily.

Alexandra Rabey (9)
Frisby CE Primary School, Melton Mowbray

Michael Jackson Dream World!

I woke up and went straight to the recording
studio. When I got there, I rushed quickly
inside. Five hours later, I had loads of money,
$5,000,000! *Ding-dong* It was a policeman. Me and
Quincy were put in cells and we were never seen
again …

Daniel Jane (9)
Frisby CE Primary School, Melton Mowbray

Alien Attack

5, 4, 3, 2, 1 - ignition. 'You ready for this dude?'
'You betcha!' Suddenly very loud smashes made
the whole shuttle tilt sideways. 'You'll never make
it to headquarters alive, never.'
'Wanna bet Gruntox?'
'Uh ow oo.'
Kaboom!
'Yes we've defeated the aliens and landed on
Mars alive!'

Rohan Edwards Cole (8)
Frisby CE Primary School, Melton Mowbray

Space

The mighty spaceship left Earth. About
two minutes after lift off the spaceship had
disappeared. Something emerged from the
clouds. It was a colossal chunk of the spaceship.
Everyone ran. The crew noticed and they started
to mend it. The ship was fixed and the mission
was complete.

Luke Chilton (8)
Frisby CE Primary School, Melton Mowbray

Humpty-Dumpty

Humpty-Dumpty sat on the brick wall, it was a sunny day, so he was happy. Suddenly he fell … *crash!* Humpty cracked his head. The ambulance took Humpty-Dumpty to hospital and it took them seven hours to fix him. After that he was back on the wall.

Thomas Mayfield (8)

Frisby CE Primary School, Melton Mowbray

Shark Pool

'We're here. Let's watch the sharks Mum. Argh!
I'm falling! Mum, save me!' I shouted as my head
got dunked under the water. 'Save me, there is a
deadly shark in the pool!'
'You don't need saving, it's a basking shark,
they're friendly!'

Archie Payne (9)
Frisby CE Primary School, Melton Mowbray

Dinosaur

'Hi!'
'Hello,' I said.
'What's that? Look, up in the sky?'
'It's a comet. Look there are two comets.'
'Argh! Run! Run for your life.' The comets glowed
in the mist. Suddenly there was a loud crash -
bang ...

Jacob Cooter (8)
Frisby CE Primary School, Melton Mowbray

The Incredible Titanic

The greatest ship set sail from Southampton. It quickly glided across the ocean with over 7,000 people aboard. *Crash!* Suddenly the Titanic hit an iceberg. Slowly it started to sink and everyone started to scream and worry. The lifeguards were quickly getting the lifeboats on the water.

James Rowell (9)
Frisby CE Primary School, Melton Mowbray

95

Death Began

Before tea the bell rang. I crept slowly to answer the door. There in front of me was a hideous-looking creature. My heart pounded as the blood dripped down its face. I rushed into the living room as it followed me. Suddenly there was a scream and silence came.

Emily Green (9)
Frisby CE Primary School, Melton Mowbray

The Walk

'The fat mouse and the thin snake went on a walk. Soon it was lunchtime and the snake was starving but the mouse had no lunch. Then about an hour later the snake got even more hungry and he nearly ate the mouse. The end,' said Mum.

Henry Murch (10)
Frisby CE Primary School, Melton Mowbray

Splash!

The mouse thought he was the monkey. He started to swing on the old branch in his cage. Suddenly *crash!* The branch snapped and he fell in his water bowl. 'Argh!' *Splash!*

Emily Voyce (8)
Frisby CE Primary School, Melton Mowbray

Goliath

Goliath chucked a wriggly worm down a deep,
dark well. Years later something was killing
people. Videos captured the snake. It was
Goliath's fault. He had metal armour and swords.
Goliath set out and fought. Every time he slashed
his sword the snake healed! Eventually parts
floated down the stream.

Curtis Machin (10)
Frisby CE Primary School, Melton Mowbray

Stop, No

'Stop, no!' But it was too late. Blue had already
leapt out the water. Magnificently he flew through
the hoop, however I only just missed it. When
I was back in the water I suddenly said, 'Blue,
never do that again.'

Lydia Harris (8)
Frisby CE Primary School, Melton Mowbray

The Big Disaster

At night people danced under the stars and moon. A sudden noise alerted the ship ... People stopped. *Crash!* The ship hit an iceberg and swayed to one side. People fell over violently. The ship was over ... it had sunk ... gone forever.

Joseph Wilford (9)
Frisby CE Primary School, Melton Mowbray

Search For Nessie The Loch Ness Monster

Two men sailed out to find Nessie. They searched
and searched till they saw something huge
floating. Then a colossal creature poked its head
out of the water. *It's Nessie,* thought the man.
Nessie flipped the boat over and the men swam
away in horror. 'Argh!' they both screamed.

Joseph Halford (9)

Frisby CE Primary School, Melton Mowbray

Stray Dog

Lights fade. Black out! Moonlight fills the sky.
Someone's in the old house. This is it. I pick up
the dog and take him inside. 'Anyone home?' I call.
'You shouldn't have come!' a voice growls.
'Here's your dog.'
'Not mine,' she hisses plunging the knife deep
into my neck …

Ellen Edwards Cole (10)
Frisby CE Primary School, Melton Mowbray

Will The Visitor Stay?

Paige was alone so she walked to the pond. In the pond the pigs were swimming and dancing in their pink bikinis. All of a sudden Nanny McPhee appeared and with one bang the pigs stopped. Paige was nervous. *Is Nanny McPhee staying?* She thought.

Heidi Dolby (11)

Frisby CE Primary School, Melton Mowbray

The Legend

It's the first time I've ever been here and I don't want to come back. But I have to do this for Firedore. I venture further into the cavern when I suddenly hear a deafening roar. It scares the life out of me yet I keep going down the cavern …

Alex Horobin (10)
Frisby CE Primary School, Melton Mowbray

The Haunted House

Bang! goes the door to the haunted house. I have a funny feeling about this house. My spine goes all shivery. I look out of the window and the swing swings. Then I hear the tap running. I turn the tap off. *Bang!* It's twelve o'clock …

Lydia Hemsley (10)
Frisby CE Primary School, Melton Mowbray

On The Run!

Tom ran, faster than he'd ever run before. 'Tom, come back,' came a rasping voice. Tom skidded round a corner and reached a dead end. 'Tom, Tom!' rasped the voice. Tom readied himself for the apparition. The rasping figure came into the light.
'There you are,' panted Tom's brother.

Samuel Thomas (10)
Frisby CE Primary School, Melton Mowbray

School Sprint!

Lucy sprinted around the school, but the figure was still following her, calling out her name! She rounded the last corner, but discovered that the exit was locked! She turned to face the figure … 'Lucy, what are you doing here?' asked Bob the school caretaker. 'Let me take you home.'

Eleanor Marles (11)
Frisby CE Primary School, Melton Mowbray

Landing On Saturn

One day in March someone flew into Saturn. He felt nervous and then he knew he was the first to get to Saturn. It felt very warm and very big and bouncy. It looked browny-green with gigantic rocky rings. He would be a millionaire now!

Victor Dexter (10)
Frisby CE Primary School, Melton Mowbray

Legend Of The Seeker

The Seeker Richard fights to stop Dorken-Roll from getting all three boxes and taking over the world. The Seeker's assisted by Raitlin and the most powerful wizard of all time -Zeer. Dorken-Roll already has two boxes, will the Seeker stop him? Who knows. Dorken-Roll or the Seeker?

Tanguy Whenham-Bossy (11)
Frisby CE Primary School, Melton Mowbray

UFO

Yesterday Becky saw a UFO, zoom across the sky! It landed in her back garden. She was alone that night, she got afraid. The aliens were green with four eyes. They came closer, then out of nowhere a dog charged and gobbled them up, that was the end of that!

Alice Coleman (11)
Frisby CE Primary School, Melton Mowbray

Freezing

Bob was freezing, he couldn't feel his feet. Barely remembering the past, Bob walked towards the rocket's window. Bob's eyes opened wider, Pluto was in front of him. Suddenly the heating turned off, the past came back to Bob, he'd crashed! The floor was scattered with gear. Where was Jim?

Katherine Halford (11)
Frisby CE Primary School, Melton Mowbray

Nose

It was a funny Monday morning and Jamie was bored, so bored his bogie that had been freshly picked was more exciting than anything in the house. Suddenly David burst out, 'You know if you pick your nose It'll fall off!' At that moment Jamie's nose fell off.

Rory Lee (10)
Frisby CE Primary School, Melton Mowbray

Narnia

I opened the door. It was really cold. I went further and further. It was getting colder and colder. Suddenly I fell on some cold white stuff. I jumped up, 'Where am I?' It looked like a whole new magical place. Suddenly I heard footsteps - there was a man ...

Millie Spencer (10)

Frisby CE Primary School, Melton Mowbray

Trapped

I am scared, so scared that I could scream! I'm
stuck under rubble and can't move. 'Ouch my leg!
I think I've cut or broken it! Oh please someone
help me. I need to live for my family.'

Ilea Cavner (10)
Frisby CE Primary School, Melton Mowbray

The Soul Stealer

Knock, knock, knock. The door creaked open,
then something appeared right in front of me.
'What are you doing?'
I'm going to take over your soul.'
'But you can't, I won't let you. Some one help me,
please help me please. Argh!' *Bang.* And that was
the end of me!

Sophia Cleaver (10)
Frisby CE Primary School, Melton Mowbray

The Horse And The Unicorn

A horse and a unicorn had a race, it was across a rainbow. The unicorn won. But the horse hurt its leg and the unicorn felt sorry. The unicorn used his horn to make the horse's leg better. They now live together on the other side of the rainbow.

Paige Gass (10)
New York Primary School, New York

The Witch And The Dragon

The witch sees a dragon. She decides to get rid
of it because she secretly is afraid of flames. She
makes a flames' potion. 'Water, rain, extinguish
the flames - fizzle, die.' She rides on her
broomstick. The flames splutter and the dragon
shrinks to the size of a pea!

Gemma Picksley (8)
New York Primary School, New York

The BFG

On a cold day giants were terrorising a town.
However the BFG was making a potion to kill
the giants. He got his blow trumpet and drizzled
the potion in it. When the BFG got to the giants
he blew the potion in their eyes and the giants
dropped dead.

Chloe Donohue (9)
New York Primary School, New York

The Dragon And The Rainbow

Long, long ago there lived a dragon. A rainbow appeared. 'I wonder what is at the end of it?' He arrived. Guess what? A pot of gold. He took it home and out popped a genie. They became friends and walked over the rainbow to start a new life together.

Melissa Picksley (10)
New York Primary School, New York

Shrek And Bob

Once upon a time there was an ogre called
Shrek and a dragon called Bob. They were worst
enemies. One day Shrek was walking in the
woods. Bob jumped out and scared Shrek; he
was being mean. Shrek's mum, Fiona, caught Bob
teasing and cast a friendship spell.

Catherine Oliver (9)
New York Primary School, New York

The Story Of The Dragon

Crack! The egg shattered. The toad touched
the ferocious dragon. A storm was beginning to
rage. *Kazoom!* The dragon glided away and got
captured by a hunter. The dragon tried to flee but
died noisily. Crowds came to look and they were
joyous.
'Cool,' someone shouted.

Leon Huang (9)
Parsons Heath CE Primary School, Colchester

Ghost House

Creak! The floorboards crackled. A flash of lightning glowed in the distance. *'Ooohhh! '* Something floated in front of Sam. *Boom!* The diamond-shaped lights and the dusty, ruined ceiling fell down onto the wooden floor. Sam ran as fast as he could out of the house. Safe to his friends.

Ryan Extance (9)
Parsons Heath CE Primary School, Colchester

The Drop

An excited couple chatted happily as they drove merrily to the shop. They crossed a bridge. There was a bang. *Click, snap* and the car dropped downwards. Suddenly the car filled with water. They were terrified. Frantically they swam out of the window to the shore. Now safe at home.

Lili Walsh (9)

Parsons Heath CE Primary School, Colchester

The Tennis Ball

Tap, tap! Someone was at the door. Dad got up. He opened the door slowly. There was nobody there. Then it started again. *Tap, tap!* Dad went to the door. Nobody there. *Tap, tap!* We all went together. There on the doorstep was a tennis ball.

Abby Constable (10)
Parsons Heath CE Primary School, Colchester

The Birthday

Pitter-patter! 'Everyone has forgotten my birthday.' *Errrrrr!* The floor creaked. 'Why is the door so bright?' He walked towards it and knocked violently. *Boom!* Lightning struck. 'Everybody in love go put your hands up, if you're in love put your hands up!' The door opened. 'Surprise!' they shouted.

Daniel Eaton (9)

Parsons Heath CE Primary School, Colchester

The Vampig

One mysterious night the vampig burst out of his pig farm. It ate all of the American vegetables, then the grim reaper killed the vampig whilst saying, 'Stop eating our vegetables, vampig.' Vampig died saying 'Why, Dracula why?'

Jesse Pavitt (9)
Parsons Heath CE Primary School, Colchester

Humpty-Dumpty

As Humpty-Dumpty struggled up the hill, he
found a wall. He jumped onto it and suddenly the
wall began to crumble beneath him. Down fell
Humpty all cracked. Poor Humpty-Dumpty. 'Help
this man up' said a sergeant. Humpty woke up,
they'd put him together again.

Chloe Webber (10)
Parsons Heath CE Primary School, Colchester

Incey Wincey Henry

Incey Wincey Henry climbed up the walls of the
mansion. Down came a cat and got stuck on his
head. Incey cried, 'Oh no my crown is gone.' He
looked down. It was on Prince Charles' head.
Now he would be the King of England.

Cameron Hurst (10)
Parsons Heath CE Primary School, Colchester

Hiccups

'I've got hiccups.' I cried.
'Hold your breath then,' replied Mum.
'I've already tried that,' I moaned.
'Try again,' Mum shouted.
'Fine.' I said annoyed. So I did but it didn't work.
'Rahhh!'
'Argh!' I screamed. 'Tom I hate you!' I said, 'but thank you, my hiccups have gone.'

Lauren Potter (10)
Parsons Heath CE Primary School, Colchester

Dark Night

Bang! Walls shook. Hovering in the doorway
stood a black figure, his breath echoed in the
empty hall. An arm reached for the light. I
wriggled under musty covers. Light flickered. I
untangled myself from the blankets.
'I'm home.' The figure declared. Relief flooded
through me.'
'Dad!'

Leanne Brunning (10)
Parsons Heath CE Primary School, Colchester

The Bee

Buzz, buzz, buzz! It stung. 'Ow, Mum!' I cried. I felt a tear coming down my eyes. The bee flew away. I screamed in pain. 'I'm allergic to bees,' so we rushed to the hospital. They gave me medicine and I recovered.

Lucy Freeman (10)
Parsons Heath CE Primary School, Colchester

The Ghost

Lucie shot out of bed. She saw something in
the corner of her eye. Nothing there. She kept
seeing it. She felt heartbeats and her blood pump.
Then she saw it. A ghost! It trapped her, she was
never to be seen again. Lost forever, vanished,
disappeared in infinity.

Zoe Beale (9)
Parsons Heath CE Primary School, Colchester

133

Halloween Night

It was pitch-black. My pointed vicious teeth
glowed in the darkness. I snuck up to the dimly lit
door. *Knock! Knock!* My cousin opened it.
'Trick or treat?' his mouth opened wide.
'*Argh!*' he screeched in fear.
'So you like my costume then?' I cried. I exploded
with laughter.

Jack Hibble (10)
Parsons Heath CE Primary School, Colchester

The Fox And The Hunter

Bang! The sound of a gun filled the air. Pete the
fox ran for his life as the hunter aimed for the
little fox. One bullet flew past his head while
another hit his bushy tail. *Come on!* he thought as
he became close to a hiding spot. Finally, safety …

Chelsea Freeman (10)
Parsons Heath CE Primary School, Colchester

My Hero

One day Dannie and Carla were walking home
when out of the bushes jumped a ... ferocious
dog! It went absolutely mental. It was barking. It
tried to attack Carla but Danni stepped in front of
her.
'Danni you saved me. You're my hero.'
'Well I'd risk my life for you!'

Abigail Stoker (11)
Parsons Heath CE Primary School, Colchester

Cheese

In a magical emerald-green forest lived an elf
who loved cheese. The elf went to the shop,
there was no cheese so he hired a boat and sailed
everywhere. He fought pirates, dwarves and
goblins. Suddenly a golden glow appeared and
took the exited elf to cheese heaven.

Laren Roper (11)

Parsons Heath CE Primary School, Colchester

The Noise Outside

The house was quiet. Everyone was asleep in their beds. Suddenly someone heard a noise outside. He looked out of his large window but there was no one there. So he looked downstairs. He saw a fully grown dragon gobbling the chicken. It saw him and he fled.

Josh Hadden (11)
Parsons Heath CE Primary School, Colchester

The Battle Royal

One foggy night a frog and T-rex battle till death.
The frog is a lot taller than the T-rex but the
T-rex has more power than the frog. The frog can
jump a lot higher so there is a massive fight. Who
do you think will win this mighty battle?

Jack Champion (11)
Parsons Heath CE Primary School, Colchester

My Chocolate Home

I dreamt my home was made of chocolate. My servant was made of chocolate! I didn't have a TV. I didn't have electricity, I didn't have a heater. If I did, my home would melt! I woke up straightaway. I found chocolate on my desk. So I ate it.

Queenet Awesu (11)

Parsons Heath CE Primary School, Colchester

Dad's Lost!

Adam was hiding. Mary was looking for him, she was getting really bored! Suddenly Adam jumped out of the wardrobe and scared her to death! They both started laughing but the problem was they lost Dad. They kept on looking but they couldn't find him! They were both extremely scared.

Millie Stoker (11)

Parsons Heath CE Primary School, Colchester

My Birthday!

Bam! I suddenly woke up. No one was there. I remembered it was my birthday. It was 7am. I went downstairs, it was pitch-black. Turned on the light, 'Surprise!' my family made a surprise. Then I found it was all a dream.

Connor Goodwin (10)
Parsons Heath CE Primary School, Colchester

Attack Of The Fluffy Monster

A fireman went rushing into a building to save
someone. Only the house wasn't burning. It just
smelt like smoke. It was dark. He couldn't see
where he was going. When he got in, a fluffy
monster came and shouted, 'Boo!' and he ran
away and was never seen again.

Marcus Fenton (11)
Parsons Heath CE Primary School, Colchester

143

The Beast

I crept slowly into the dark, deserted house. I had come to retrieve my ball. 'Aeorugh!' I heard a sudden roar, a figure leapt towards me. Its twisted face was covered in blood. I screamed, and ran for my life. Suddenly I collapsed, the beast feasted on my screaming body.

Liam McKenna (10)

Parsons Heath CE Primary School, Colchester

The Chocolate Angel

In Heaven there was an angel called Melanie. She came down from Heaven and made parents give their children chocolate. After two months God fired her. She made all the children fat. So she found billions of juicy grapes and got her job back. Now she is the grape fairy.

Lucy Nobile (9)
Parsons Heath CE Primary School, Colchester

Halloween Night

I was asleep. A big bang came. I woke up as fast
as I could. I realised it was the door. I was just
going to watch TV but I peeked outside …
'Boo!' It was a flesh-eating monster. It laughed
loudly. So did I.

Luke Mayhew (9)
Parsons Heath CE Primary School, Colchester

Magic Angels

Bang! The thunder in Heaven cracked. I thought I
saw an angel hovering in the distance. As I looked
across I saw not one but three angels. They came
flying towards me. The angels picked me up and
took me back home. Was it a dream?

Shawn Banks (10)

Parsons Heath CE Primary School, Colchester

147

Angel

Songs of praise were sung as an angel floated down elegantly from Heaven. She came face to face with the enemy. She took the first shot with a golden beam ray. It creaked loudly but it didn't seem to hurt. She knew this was her last chance to fight Halloween.

Rebecca Edwardson (9)

Parsons Heath CE Primary School, Colchester

Bloodthirsty Flesh Eater

I was alone in the hallway listening to a mysterious noise. I trembled in fear. I felt a shiver down my spine. *Raarh!'* A lean figure with blood-dripping fangs spotted me! I looked round, finding an exit. *Pounce!* I was cornered. 'So you liked my Halloween suit?' he cried.

Kyle Nuttall (10)
Parsons Heath CE Primary School, Colchester

The Butterfly

Becky skipped through fields of flowers. A butterfly drifted towards her. Suddenly she remembered her grandad's warning, 'Be careful with butterflies,' but she wasn't scared of this delicate one. Becky sat by a tree, the butterfly followed her. It got bigger and bigger, then Becky disappeared. Except for her spirit.

India Hood (10)

Parsons Heath CE Primary School, Colchester

The Scare

'I don't have any friends,' mumbled the alien. The problem was he had fluffy eyes and ears and a cute grin. Everyone picked on him because he wasn't scary. He looked at his map. 'Let's go to Earth.' He said his goodbyes. He knew he'd be safe on Earth.

Charlie Shave (9)
Parsons Heath CE Primary School, Colchester

Christmas Eve

It was cold, dim, and gloomy. Darkness filled the house except for the gaps of glistening light that shone through a bedroom door. Katie waited timidly for him. *Boom!* A noise from the living room, who was it? She crept downstairs. There in front was a shiny, red bottom, Santa!

Leannon Buy (10)
Parsons Heath CE Primary School, Colchester

Space Shuttle

Saucers fall out of the sky. Lights flash. They crawl forward. Green, brown, pink, yellow. They come closer, closer to me. *Zap!* A metal pellet zooms at my head. Luckily they miss. I run away but they're too fast, I've been shot. I'm now down to the floor.

Emma Wright (10)
Parsons Heath CE Primary School, Colchester

153

The Bloodthirsty Vampire

One stormy night there was a mysterious,
spooky, haunted house, no one dared to go
inside.
One night someone went inside. To their
amazement they saw a … bloodthirsty vampire!
They were scared stiff! Just then the vampire
turned into a pitch-black bat!
It was all a dream!

Izzy Waddington (7)
Red Hill Primary School, Chislehurst

154

Mr Pea

Mr Pea walked down a sunny street. Suddenly a tall man picked him up, he was surprised and scared. The tall man nibbled on him but Mr Pea was not tasty. The man took him to his house and left him on the dirty table. Mr Pea hopped home.

Phoebe Lands (8)
Red Hill Primary School, Chislehurst

A Dog And Halloween Treats

A man called Ben had a dog, his marvellous
dog could talk. But when it was Halloween the
fantastic and cool dog couldn't talk at all. Ben
tried hard for him to talk. Ben gave his dog some
special Halloween doggy treats. Suddenly his dog
started to talk again.

Chyna Star McAvoy (8)
Red Hill Primary School, Chislehurst

My Loss

I have visions of death, destruction, loss. I lie in
bed at night, tossing; turning. I can't sleep. The
visions are nightmares … nightmares beyond
man! Man cannot see these. I am different.
My dad says they're not real … but I know,
somewhere, there's a world, crying out for
help …

Emily Bown (10)
Rothley CE Primary School, Leicester

Stranded!

Washed ashore on a scorching, sunny sandbed
- I carefully rose spitting out seawater! *Crunch!*
startling me out of my skin, wondering what it
was, I stepped closer. A rustling ahead alerted me;
a pair of beady eyes stared right at me. My heart
stopped beating, the tension was immense ...
'Cat!'

Chloe Hall (10)
Rothley CE Primary School, Leicester

A Day In The Life Of Angus Unlucky!

Born on Friday 13th, Angus Unlucky's life is always eventful. He's the world's unluckiest person! Just this morning (a crisp, clear one) he slipped on ice, his car broke down on the motorway and he lost his wallet! He's as unlucky as the number thirteen. Will his luck ever change … ?

James Dudfield (10)
Rothley CE Primary School, Leicester

Truly Unbelievable!

Lying on the smooth, sandy shore gazing deep
into shimmering night skies, I watched intensely
the bright, glistening, glowing stars, like diamonds
in an expensive jeweller's window - *woosh!* There
before my very own eyes was an amazing sight
... unbelievable ... surreal ... A shooting star ...
Wow ... a magic ice cube moment.

Kizzy Simpson (11)
Rothley CE Primary School, Leicester

Scared Stiff

My heart pounded rapidly; I clasped my hands in anguish. Scarcely breathing I looked around cautiously! Suddenly sinister eyes emerged mysteriously from behind a tree! I felt uneasy, wondering if I should turn back, when a figure sprang out at me.
'Surprise!' My brother laughed. 'Isn't my Halloween costume great?'

Emma Hope Bardsley (10)
Rothley CE Primary School, Leicester

Surprise!

Creeping quietly down the old wooden staircase,
we hid behind the new black sofa. The shiny
paper, heavy and lumpy glistened and rustled.
Suddenly mum walked down the familiar staircase
- *creak, creak* - yawning sleepily.
'Happy Mother's Day Mum,' we all shouted
noisily.
'Wow what a wonderful surprise!' Mum tearfully
shrieked.

Hannah Carpenter (11)
Rothley CE Primary School, Leicester

Freakout!

Whoah, whoah went a strange sound. Kate started
to shiver. 'W-w-hat's that noise? I'm really scared.'
Kate walked closer and closer to the noise. 'Argh!
Argh! Argh! What's that?' Kate ran to the kitchen.
'There's ghosts!' So Kate ran upstairs and went
for some beauty sleep. 'Phew!'

Niamh Ferris (8)
St Peter Chanel RC Primary School, Sidcup

Missing Monkey

The zoo had loads of monkeys. A baby monkey swung away. Lots of people were trying to find it. A little girl said, 'I found the missing baby monkey.'

No one believed her and laughed. 'You live in the city.'

The next day she brought it back to the zoo.

Holly Jotham (8)
St Peter Chanel RC Primary School, Sidcup

The Haunted House

One mysterious day I was walking home with
Shay. We had so much fun in the park. We
went into our house and suddenly we heard a
creak. But no one was home. So we screamed,
'Aaaaaaaah!'
'I'm very, very scared, Shay, are you?'
'Yes, I'm scared too Molly.'

Molly Lowe (8)
St Peter Chanel RC Primary School, Sidcup

The Birthday Party

I'm a pretty girl called Shay. My friend Orla was having a birthday party. I asked, 'Can I put a party on for you?'
'Yes you can, I'll help you.'
The day came and Orla was excited. I thought it was going to go terribly wrong. 'This isn't right. Whoops!'

Orla Ferris (8)
St Peter Chanel RC Primary School, Sidcup

The Haunted House

As I opened the door I heard a creak. It was very spooky. Then I saw a pot of green gooey stuff. I put my hand in. It felt like sticky slime. Then I walked upstairs. 1 step, 2 step, then *creak*. *'Argh!'*

Shay Stewart-Poynter (8)
St Peter Chanel RC Primary School, Sidcup

The Castle

One day there was a boy named Charlie. He went in a spooky castle. He heard spooky noises and he thought the floor was a bit bouncy. Then someone turned the lights on and Charlie realised that it was a Halloween party and that the floor was a bouncy castle.

Callum Roberts (8)
St Peter Chanel RC Primary School, Sidcup

The Midnight Scream!

Kelly woke up. She heard a scream. Suddenly a movement. There was a bang at the door and she dived under the quilt.
'Did I wake you?' It was John or Scarlet crying for milk. Dad stepped in the room. Kelly hugged teddy, turned over and went to sleep.

Sophie Douglas (7)
St Peter Chanel RC Primary School, Sidcup

The House!

As I opened the creaky door my head started to shake. I got jelly legs. It was terrifying! I stepped on a wooden plank. *Creak!* 'Anybody there?' I walked just one more step and another and another. *Crrr!* Phew! Just another plank. 1 step, 2 step.
'*Argh!* Someone help!'

Lucy Dixon (8)
St Peter Chanel RC Primary School, Sidcup

Grimy House

One day Adrian was walking home. He was very excited because it was his birthday that day. He had asked for a surprise party. He walked into the house and saw it was grimy. He switched on the light. Oh my! It was gooey and sticky …

Matthew Clarke (7)
St Peter Chanel RC Primary School, Sidcup

Darkest Night

It was midnight. I thought to myself *Why am I awake?* I heard the bell ring. My sister was now awake, and crying. I got up, put my dressing gown on, and ran downstairs. I walked down after and opened the door but there was nothing there. How spooky! Wow!

Jude Platton (7)

St Peter Chanel RC Primary School, Sidcup

What A Surprise!

One night Jessica was returning home from the
pub. Her parents went out! Meanwhile her aunty
stayed! The house was dark. No one was there.
Jessica felt a shiver run down her spine!
'Boo!' Her aunty jumped up behind her!
'Arrr! Help! Help! What a huge surprise that
Halloween!

Izzy Venables (7)
St Peter Chanel RC Primary School, Sidcup

173

The Large Surprise

I was in bed but it was 1am. So I went back
to sleep. Then I woke up and *rip!* Why does it
happen to me? I could not sleep but then my
family said, 'Surprise!'

Jaime Jaramillo Fernandez (8)
St Peter Chanel RC Primary School, Sidcup

The Haunted Castle

Once there was a slimy castle with a wicked witch and wizard. Also there was one lovely girl and her twin brother. One of them brought a tarantula and it started to talk! He said, 'What are you doing?' Wow! How amazing!

Hannah Louise Campbell (7)
St Peter Chanel RC Primary School, Sidcup

Untitled

One day a boy went to the park, there were sunflowers growing. He heard something. He looked at one of the sunflowers, it was talking to him. The sunflower was talking to him! It said, 'Pick me off the ground, and I'll be able to walk and talk.'
'OK.'

Morgan Nicklin (8)
St Peter Chanel RC Primary School, Sidcup

The Scary House

One day Adnan walked into this very dark house.
When you touched the door it fell down. In the
house there was nothing. In a room there was
a horrible monster. It had a big mole on its nose
and black fur. Also the windows were all smashed
up.

Euan Edwards (8)
St Peter Chanel RC Primary School, Sidcup

The Horrible Dentist

One day a little girl was playing in the park. Then she saw a ball that she wanted to kick. So she did. It went over a horrible dentist's house. She went to get it. The horrible dentist said, 'Come in.' So she did. The dentist pulled her teeth out!

Chloe Kearney-Adams (8)
St Peter Chanel RC Primary School, Sidcup

My Tomatoes

The boy planted his seeds in the pots and waited each day for his plants to appear. He came home from school to find they were floppy. He was sad. He watered them and hoped they would grow. Then he looked one sunny morning to find green tomatoes. He's happy!

Andrew Alford (8)
St Peter Chanel RC Primary School, Sidcup

The Egg Hunt

It was the day of the exciting egg hunt. Mum was
hosting the event. My friends were hunting too.
We all ran off into the woods! I found a small egg.
I went back. The egg hatched, it was a pocket
dragon. The dragon became my friend.
'Daddy, daddy!'

Charlie Wilkinson (8)
St Peter Chanel RC Primary School, Sidcup

Victory

With the Spanish boats getting nearer, Nelson had to think fast. He ordered the fuses on all cannons. Suddenly one bang after another the cannons fired, the smoke was everywhere. Lord Nelson saw the Spanish boats had been sunk, another victory, just.

Daniel Hammond-Cortes (9)
St Peter Chanel RC Primary School, Sidcup

Ghosts Or Is It Real?

Kylie was shivering, she slowly crept into the dark deserted house. No wait! There was light. She saw the shadowy figure approaching. Kylie was scared. She opened the door then … the figure jumped out at her; it was her lost brother. How happy she was to see him again!

Jiawen Guo (9)
St Peter Chanel RC Primary School, Sidcup

The Face Of The Enemy

I awaited the Colonel's orders. The atmosphere was extremely tense. Then I heard it, 'Go, go, go!' We all ran frantically over the top, yelling and screaming. Then, as if the Devil had woken, the enemy charged out of their trench! Finally I saw my enemy face to face …

Samuel Carter (9)
St Peter Chanel RC Primary School, Sidcup

183

What A Nightmare

There was a monkey called Peanuts who was playing in the trees when he heard a rumbling noise coming towards him. Nearer it came, he was scared. He put his hands over his head and saw a tractor. He screamed. Peanuts woke up, realising it was a nightmare.

Yolanda Paasche (9)

St Peter Chanel RC Primary School, Sidcup

The Lost Horse

The horse was lost and he couldn't find his mum.
He ran around the field looking everywhere, but
she was gone. He was very sad but then he saw
a lady horse called Annie and he ran quickly up to
her. They then became friends and lived happily
ever after.

Martine Grzybkowski (8)
St Peter Chanel RC Primary School, Sidcup

185

Disco Fever

I opened a bright pink door. As I walked in I found someone with an Afro dancing to 'We Will Rock You'. The music was so loud it made me jump as soon as I opened the door. It was a very, very big surprise to me.

Hawa Alpha (9)
St Peter Chanel RC Primary School, Sidcup

The Ugly, Ugly Monster

The duvet was pulled tightly over my head, there
was a loud screech. I pulled the pillow over my
head, my eyes peeping. Suddenly I saw an ugly
face with hair sticking, mascara dripping down her
face. I screamed.
'Breakfast is ready.' It became clear, it was only
my mum.

Adam Sangster (8)
St Peter Chanel RC Primary School, Sidcup

187

My Nightmare Dream

I was going to the park, when I passed a
mansion. It looked like a haunted house and I
wondered what was in there. So I went inside,
the floorboards creaked then suddenly I heard a
noise. Frightened I tried to leave. All the doors
closed, then I awoke.

Seónaid Divers (9)
St Peter Chanel RC Primary School, Sidcup

The Lingering Shadow Of Fear

The stream looked like a silvery snake when the full moon shone upon it. The woods echoed with the sound of the wolves. Suddenly a light flickered in the distance near the old abandoned cottage. A black shadow appeared at the window, then disappeared in a cloud of green mist.

Larissa D'Cruze (8)

St Peter Chanel RC Primary School, Sidcup

Victory

Peter and Matthew hear the news that a sea monster has taken all the water from the UK. They think they can help. They get into suits and fight the sea monster, Matthew and Peter win. They win victory. No one knows their real identity because they are disguised brilliantly.

Adrian Vishal Antony Pillai (9)
St Peter Chanel RC Primary School, Sidcup

Sticks And Stones

I was lying on a big cold table, it started to move
up and down. I saw an image of a skeleton, I
started to shiver, there was another bright flash.
Eyes closed tightly. I kept perfectly still, frightened
to move a muscle. The X-ray doctor said, 'It's not
broken.'

Luke Sangster (8)
St Peter Chanel RC Primary School, Sidcup

Tom And The Dragon

Tom was walking in the forest when he suddenly
stopped. There was a big purple dragon standing
in front of him.
'Hello,' said the dragon, 'Jump on my back.' Tom
and the dragon flew over the mountains.
Tom heard a voice below calling, 'Tom, wake up.'
He had been dreaming!

Tegan Rickwood (8)
St Peter Chanel RC Primary School, Sidcup

My Prayer For A Good Recycling

One Saturday I went with my father to recycling in my neighbourhood and saw fantastic things like people wouldn't even think about recycling back home. I told my mother what I saw and I told her that recycling was the best thing we could do for the planet and the world.

Isabella Gaviria (8)

St Peter Chanel RC Primary School, Sidcup

Tsunami

I was trapped beneath the gigantic waves. I tried to find something to keep me afloat, there was nothing. My last chance was around the corner. I made a grab for it, but missed. Suddenly there was a huge splash. I was at the end of the water rapid ride.

Zak Conquest (8)

St Peter Chanel RC Primary School, Sidcup

A Miracle Day For United!

The school football pitch was getting cold. It was neck and neck between Sidcup United and Hull. It was a Cup match. Just then Mike got the ball and had a long distance shot! With one minute left he scored! Sidcup United won the Cup. That was a great day!

George Wood (9)
St Peter Chanel RC Primary School, Sidcup

Our Visit To The Pet Shop

I went to the pet shop with my cousin. She was holding a furry hamster in her hands. 'He's so quick, I have to sit down.' Then he quickly jumped off her lap. 'Oh what are we going to do?' asked my cousin, then he ran back to us.

Georgia Lilly Beaumont (8)
St Peter Chanel RC Primary School, Sidcup

Untitled

One day I was at the forest and I heard a noise in a cave. So then I went inside the cave and found a big brown grizzly bear. It attacked me so I ran away very fast.

James Alderson (8)
St Peter Chanel RC Primary School, Sidcup

A Fun Day At The Seaside

I went to the seaside and had an ice cream that was yummy. I saw a very big shell and a crab was under it. I saw a jellyfish, I was scared but it didn't get me. It was a great day that I loved and enjoyed with my friends.

Melissa Hall (9)
St Peter Chanel RC Primary School, Sidcup

Spooky House

Sunday Jos went to a house which was spooky.
Jos was scared and frightened. There were traps
but Jos didn't fall for the traps. Then two doors
opened after that. Jos screamed. There was a
person behind the door.
'Help!'
'Surprise!' it was his mother.

Jeswin Jekson (8)
St Peter Chanel RC Primary School, Sidcup

New School

I went to a new school. I was pretty scared
at first, but I got used to it, and made loads of
friends. I was really pleased. When I went home
I told my mum. She thought it was a miracle! It
must be my lucky day! Can't wait for tomorrow!

Lina Slamani (11)

St Vincent's RC Primary School, Dagenham

I Want To Go Shopping

'Mum I have to go shopping today.'
'No I told you, you're grounded,' said Mum.
'But I already told my friends though, it's just not fair.'
'I don't care, you're not going anywhere,' said Mum.
'Please Mum,' I beg.
'OK but as long as you behave with your friends.'
'OK.'

Sonzinia Chammas (10)
St Vincent's RC Primary School, Dagenham

The Run

The bushes and trees surrounded me, where would I turn? Spiders and foxes in dark holes, watching my every move. I've gone too far now, I need to get back! Cold and windy weather makes me sick. Running back, no delay, I've escaped, finally! What a big garden I have!

Desola Oguntoyinbo
St Vincent's RC Primary School, Dagenham

Goldilocks And The Alien

Goldilocks wandered into the woods one day.
She came across a house and went in. She saw
a very tall chair and she wondered how anyone
could get onto it. Just then she heard a creak on
the floor. She saw an alien and she ran all the way
home.

Kiera Fade
St Vincent's RC Primary School, Dagenham

Untitled

Terrible news broke my heart. My parents were getting an annulment. Hoping for less stress, they just heaped on more. Choosing who I want to stay with. I chose my aunt. It was hard to stay with them now. They ruined my hope for all of us. Our future together!

Kaye Lagmay

St Vincent's RC Primary School, Dagenham

Spain!

Why do my parents always ruin my life? I have to move to a new country, I don't know anyone there! We have to move to Spain! What do my parents think I'm supposed to do? Say olé and clap my hands? But I'll give it a go! Bye-bye!

Erin Curtin (11)
St Vincent's RC Primary School, Dagenham

Untitled

'Jamie, come down for breakfast, Jamie get up
you don't want to be late for your big football
match!'
'Alright, I'm getting up, stop ruining my life.'
As I went downstairs I made myself toast and she
kissed me on the cheek and said, 'Have a lovely
day at school.'

Sami Uddin

St Vincent's RC Primary School, Dagenham

Born For Skills!

The ball was in the air. Simon had his back to the goal. He knew he had to try it. If he pulled it off, if he scored with an overhead kick in front of everyone, Sion knew it would be one of the best moments of his life.

Richie Itonga
St Vincent's RC Primary School, Dagenham

Untitled

Where am I? In space, on Earth, where? So here
I am in my room but why do I feel different? I
usually feel bored and stubborn, but I actually feel
different. Oh my is that my sister? It is!
'Hi' she said. I have to get out of here!

Claudia Gega
St Vincent's RC Primary School, Dagenham

Tim's Surprise Birthday Party

It was Tim's birthday party and he was so happy because it was his birthday. His mum gave him so many presents and he had his birthday in Kid's Kingdom. Then he had fish and chips and then he went home, opened his presents and went to bed.

Jessica Jennifer Fernandes (11)
St Vincent's RC Primary School, Dagenham

Goldilocks And The Three People

Once upon a time there lived three people,
Mama, Papa and Bob. They lived deep in the
forest. One day a bear with blonde pigtails
knocked on the door. No one answered. So
Goldilocks went in and took the porridge. She
nibbled at the porridge for ten years. Naughty
girl!

Nina Bourgeois-Royer (11)
St Vincent's RC Primary School, Dagenham

My Silly Little Brother

I was in the garden playing my ball. I heard a
massive roar, turned around but there was
nobody there. I went into the shed and heard a
squeak. I turned on the lamp, nothing but empty
space. I went outside and caught my brother
giggling behind the blue shed.

Chernai Joseph (10)
St Vincent's RC Primary School, Dagenham

Untitled

In my house it's a struggle to survive, it's tough and no fun. It all started when my brother joined rugby. He was hanging with his team, he treated me like rubbish until … I got fed up of it. At home I leapt from the chair and hit him badly.

Klesha Darroux (11)
St Vincent's RC Primary School, Dagenham

Concert Disaster!

Ring ring. I picked the phone up, it was my best friend, she said 'Do you want to go to the concert in town today?'
'OK' I said. Later on at the concert there was a big bang. They said that there were technical difficulties, so we went home.

Elana Gomez (10)
St Vincent's RC Primary School, Dagenham

Bad Dreams

It was a dark, dark night. It was cold, damp and very quiet. Something, a creature, moved under the moonlight. You could see the shadows. It went around crushing everything in its path. 'It' came closer and closer towards my house, until *Bamm!* I realised it was only a dream.

Jonathan Meheux (10)
St Vincent's RC Primary School, Dagenham

The Witch

There I was face to face with a real life witch. She was really spotty, had a big nose and was green all over. But she was really nice. She offered some milk and cookies and a blanket, but then she took off her mask; it was my big sister.

Brendan Reilly

St Vincent's RC Primary School, Dagenham

Untitled

New school, first day. Nervous is today's feeling.
I'm here with nobody that I know. Everyone
dislikes me including teachers. My head teacher
likes me. Break: everyone avoids me, same as
lunch. Even lessons, especially paired work, I feel
like an outcast. This will happen again. I hate this
day!

Victoria Robles

St Vincent's RC Primary School, Dagenham

In The Crowded Shop

Birds tweeted, bunnies hopped, cats purred, dogs
growled. It felt like I was in a jungle - or even a
zoo! So many pets to choose from - I couldn't
decide! But there in the far end corner, a cute
white puppy lay in a glass cage sleeping. I chose
my pet ...

Jessica Manuel
St Vincent's RC Primary School, Dagenham

Everything Is Boring

I'm fifteen and I live in Twinkle Town. Not! I live in Brighton and it's boring. So I'm having a party and it's going to be great. Mum and Dad are out of town! Party on. What happens if something goes wrong?
Sadly Mum doesn't go. Party off!

Reanne Lord-Simpson (11)
St Vincent's RC Primary School, Dagenham

My Teacher Is A Monster From A Greek Myth

I was a normal kid, going to school, getting kicked out every single time. But this year, I witnessed something that changed my life forever. On a school trip, in my sixth grade, my teacher, Mrs Dodds, called me into a quiet room and she turned into a hideous monster.

Raphael Omobolaji Elewe
St Vincent's RC Primary School, Dagenham

Bonfire

The bonfire was raging, Guy Fawkes toppled from his perch high above. The flames engulfed everything and nothing could be seen except the embers flying high. The ashes were as black as night and the charred wood fell to the blackened ground below.

Kyle English (11)
Studfall Junior School, Corby

Spooky Schools

Monday morning, I was walking to school in the dull weather. Once I got to the gate, I stepped into the classroom and saw children walking through walls and ceilings. I had strange feelings. I ran for my life; I was too late. They dragged me far away from school.

Ashley Zorrilla (10)
Studfall Junior School, Corby

The Laughing Waves

Bradley ran across the beach, his feet splashing in the water. He finally felt happy - for once, but not for long. As he stared out to sea, it crashed towards him and pulled him in. Bradley struggled, but was quickly dragged in. He drowned as the sea laughed after him.

Stacey Stratford (11)
Studfall Junior School, Corby

Weird Or What?

Tom was taking a stroll in the park when suddenly
a green monkey landed at his feet. It roared at
him, ran on the road, jumped in front of a car and
killed itself. Tom just stood there in shock. He
didn't know what to do. Weird or what?

Ben McLean (11)
Studfall Junior School, Corby

A Sack Full Of Trouble

There was a frantic rapping on the front door.
A police siren sounded, coming closer down my
street. The door opened; a desperate-looking
man stumbled in, tossed me a sack and hurried
into my back garden. Everything happened
lightning fast. That's how I made headline news
the following day!

Imogen Cory (11)
Studfall Junior School, Corby

The Abandoned Mansion

'No!' screamed Jimmy as his friends booted his
football over the abandoned mansion's wall.
His friends told him to go and get it, so Jimmy
sprinted up the path. He kicked in the door and
strolled inside. 'Argh!' screeched Jimmy's voice as
a skull rolled out of the front door.

Cameron Harry Murray (11)
Studfall Junior School, Corby

A New Girl!

Luke just took one glance at her and he knew she
had to be the one. There was a new girl in school.
Her name was Lucy. The teacher asked, 'Who
would like to show Lucy around school?'
Luke pushed his hand up. 'I will,' whispered Luke.
Lucy just smiled …

Samantha Loveday (11)
Studfall Junior School, Corby

Springy Hair

There was a boy who didn't want to have his hair cut - but his parents made him. He had an extremely scruffy dog.
One day - at the barbers - he was having his hair cut when it suddenly hopped off his head and out the door!
'Fooled you!' the boy said.

Sam Mears (11)
Studfall Junior School, Corby

227

Bedtime Is Not Nice

I wake up at midnight and I know I am not alone.
The shadows on the wall scare me. The noises
I hear are making me jump out of my skin. My
heart pounds like a drum inside my chest. There's
a knot in my stomach. '*Hooray!* It's morning,
great.'

Beth Smith (10)
Studfall Junior School, Corby

The Arrival

Kayleigh and Jacob were overwhelmed as they
waited in the reception area of the hospital. They
were waiting for their dad to call them to go in.
After forty long minutes, their dad emerged from
the room ahead and told them they could go and
see their newly arrived siblings.

Aimee Foster (11)
Studfall Junior School, Corby

229

Night In The Graveyard

As the night came in the graveyard, a frightening sound came from a cracked gravestone. The sound got louder. Soon, the gravestone opened and a strange body stepped out. The figure walked into the night as the rest came, stumbled into the city, and screams started to sound.

Bethan McIntosh (11)

Studfall Junior School, Corby

An Amazing Discovery

It was Saturday evening and me and my mates
were up in the woods. We set up a course for a
big race. I went to the end to see who would win.
On the way, I stumbled into a ditch in the shape
of a dinosaur footprint!

Ricky Carr
Studfall Junior School, Corby

A Night At Aunt Ruby's

Lea, an average girl, was sentenced to her aunt
Ruby's house for the weekend. But what she
didn't know was what her aunt was really like.
The night was dim, the silence was unpredictable.
The timing was unsatisfying. Her aunt entered the
room with a craving for human flesh.

Meg McGivern (10)
Studfall Junior School, Corby

Untitled

Nigel peered out of the window, only to find the
boy he was hiding from. A bully was after Nigel.
He hid in his bedroom, but it was no use - Mum
let the bully in. At that moment, Nigel closed his
eyes and jumped out of the window.

Stewart Ralph Andrew Morrison (11)
Studfall Junior School, Corby

Chloe Underground

Once upon a time there lived a girl called Chloe.
She lived with her mother in a little house. One
day Chloe went out in the garden to pick some
flowers, but then she was zapped underground.
Suddenly she saw a ghost and started to run…

Sarah Gunenc (8)
Studfall Junior School, Corby

Marina Gets Lost

Once, long ago, there lived a mermaid, her name
was Marina. One day Marina's mum told her
to go to the bottom of the sea to collect shells.
When she arrived she couldn't remember the
way home so she started to cry. Just then she saw
a shark …

Alice Scott (8)
Studfall Junior School, Corby

Untitled

One day there was a haunted house. No one would go near it but Jack was just moving from New York and for some odd reason he bought it. That night he woke up at midnight, all he could hear was '*Whoo!*' Then a ghost appeared.

Graham Long (8)
Studfall Junior School, Corby

In The Jungle

The jungle was as dark as the night sky, every animal was awake. Suddenly they heard a noise again and again. Then they all saw some legs and a red cape, it was Little Red Riding Hood, looking for monkeys. Then a monkey jumped on her head …

Rachel Stratford (8)
Studfall Junior School, Corby

The Mermaid Girl

One fine day a little girl called Amy was going on holiday to Majorca. When they got there Amy begged to go swimming so they did. Amy dived in and she was a mermaid in the sea. She was swimming with fish and dolphins jumping up and down. Yay Amy!

Ella Hill
Studfall Junior School, Corby

House Of Terror

In a haunted house there lived a boy called Tyler.
One dark night he heard someone scratching
at the door. No one was there. He closed the
door, and heard chains clanking. Still no one was
there. The third time, he saw a mysterious shape
disappear, was it a ghost?

Nicole Ford (7)
Studfall Junior School, Corby

239

Out Of Space

In space a little alien named Zog lived on a bright
red planet called Mars. One day at night-time Zog
saw a rocket zoom past a shooting star which
landed behind the little cottage he lives in. Zog
ran around his cottage and saw the rocket.

Kiarna Chan (8)
Studfall Junior School, Corby

A Magic Cave

In a magic cave underground there lived a
monster called Jack. Jack loved to eat worms.
One day Jack heard a sound, it was very shocking,
so Jack went to see what it was. When he got
there, there were people and he ended up in the
greasy zoo park.

Ben Cory
Studfall Junior School, Corby

241

The Underwater Castle

Once there was a beautiful castle, in there lived a mermaid. The castle was lovely and well built. A fearsome shark appeared and was crossing into the walls of the castle. Then the mermaid's octopus came and killed the shark. They all lived happily ever after in the castle.

Abbi McKay (8)
Studfall Junior School, Corby

Jungle Bridge

One day Cheetah went on a long bridge and
Cheetah was only small. So that's why he didn't
know it was broken. Halfway there was a clink
but he didn't hear it. Suddenly all the steps fell off
then Eagle saved him. Cheetah learned his lesson.
'I hate coming here.'

Jack Lawlor (7)
Studfall Junior School, Corby

Horror House

One day there lived a man. The man lived in a
cottage. He liked spending time with relatives.
One day he accidentally fell over. A ghost broke
his fall proudly. It was his brother Callum.
'Callum.' The man felt very, very happy. Callum
came back with his relatives.

Logan McGreevy (7)
Studfall Junior School, Corby

Space Fright

One day a man, Max, decided to buy a rocket.
Then he shot into space. It took a while to get
there. When he got there he saw the moon, it
had a face on it. Suddenly an alien came by! *'Argh!'*
He screamed, so he went back to Earth.

Harry Reynolds
Studfall Junior School, Corby

Jungle Crazy!

One crazy morning in the jungle, Hippo was sleeping, Tiger was munching and the monkeys were climbing the trees. The afternoon was quickly upon them. Tiger had finished chomping, Hippo was now wide awake and the monkeys had stopped climbing. Suddenly Tiger heard a noise. Was it his tummy rumbling?

Taylor Moss (8)
Studfall Junior School, Corby

Untitled

Once upon a time there was a worm that acted like a human. One day Worm wanted some gold, so he went underground. He got a shovel and dug with all his might! Suddenly Worm forgot he was only a worm and a human came and squashed him.

Jack Lappin (8)
Studfall Junior School, Corby

247

The Jungle That Plays Tricks

One day the jungle was quiet which is the best time for Cheetah to play his tricks. So first he went to Hippo and put blue liquid in the river. 'Ill get Cheetah,' said Hippo. Hippo put a bit of meat in a cage. On the cage was red paint …

Louise Perry
Studfall Junior School, Corby

Space Mania

In outer space there were two Zog aliens Zip and
Zog. All day, every day, they were making trouble.
One day they decided they would do something
bad. They took the engine out of a spaceship.
When the astronaut came to drive it, it wouldn't
work at all.

Hannah Fox (8)
Studfall Junior School, Corby

A Rocky Tunnel

One stormy day on a beach a little dwarf decided to go underground. He walked in a tunnel. He found an exit but it was a trap! He fell in another door, he fell down a tilting path. When he got to the bottom he found an exit. 'Yes!'

Rhys Beard (8)
Studfall Junior School, Corby

Terrifying House

One terrifying night a young boy called Jack went into the terrifying house and saw a ghost. The ghost chased him round the whole house. Then suddenly Jack fell out the window and went back home. He fell asleep. Later he went back to the house and it wasn't there.

Jude Severn (8)
Studfall Junior School, Corby

251

The Jungle Rush

The jungle was calm. Tiger was sleeping, the trees were still and Monkey was swinging through the ropes. Suddenly a noise came from far ahead. The noise came closer and closer. The Tiger woke up and yawned, What's that?' It was a herd of elephants rushing home for tea.

Ashleigh Wilson (8)
Studfall Junior School, Corby

Max's Vision

Once in an old, spooky house lived a ghost. His name was Max. One night Max had a horrible vision. It was about his brother's death. When he woke up he thought about the vision again. Day after day Max had nightmares. Then he realised he needn't worry!

Tyler Fehres (8)
Studfall Junior School, Corby

A Journey In Outer Space

In outer space there's a man called Steven. As he was flying past Mars he saw tons of aliens shooting out a crater. And they didn't stop! He had to do something. He saw an asteroid and he grabbed it and put it in the crater. They stopped.

Daniel Burt

Studfall Junior School, Corby

The Stranger On Mars

Space was as dark as a monster's blood. Boxo was a little alien who lived on Mars. One day he heard a bang! He said, 'What was that?' Suddenly there was a creature coming onto Mars. Boxo was worried. It turned out to be a little poodle.

Heather McCafferty (7)
Studfall Junior School, Corby

255

Biscuit Mystery

As I walked up the creaking stairs the door opened slightly. I looked around the door but nobody was there. I made my way to the kitchen, mischievously opened the huge tin. Suddenly I heard a noise.

'Put that biscuit down,' shouted Mum. 'It's time for tea.'

Chelsea Leam (11)

Swanwick Primary School, Alfreton

A Cold Hungry Night

It was a freezing pitch-black night when there was a knock at the door that seemed to echo around the house. It frightened me. Who could be banging at my door so loudly? I nervously peeped through the small spyhole. Thank goodness for that! It was the pizza man.

Rosie Poxon (10)
Swanwick Primary School, Alfreton

The Hitman

A freezing sensation tingled down her spine. She stopped suddenly as her blood ran cold. She knew he had found her. Her heart beat loudly in her chest as she fought her emotions. She turned slowly to see her little brother throwing another perfect snowball in her direction.

Lydia Jepson (11)
Swanwick Primary School, Alfreton

Don't Talk, Kiss Me!

Romeo and Juliet longed for each other's hearts but their parents had other plans. They were not allowed to talk to each other ever again. So they kissed.

'Why are you near that boy?' said Juliet's mother.
'You said we weren't allowed to talk, not kiss!'

Katy Bowmer (11)
Swanwick Primary School, Alfreton

Untitled

As soon as I walked in the house, I darted into the
bathroom, suddenly there was a loud bang! The
hairs on the back of my head stood on end. The
door started to slowly open. A hand appeared
around the door.
'Hi love, have you had a good day?'

Trish Mukura (11)
Swanwick Primary School, Alfreton

The Door

The doorbell rang, I slowly made my way down the cobwebbed stairs. Suddenly the door handle moved up and down. Slowly I turned the key and looked around. No one was there, stepping outside I heard someone coming up the drive. 'Hi love, stick the kettle on,' said Mum.

Ewan Snow (10)
Swanwick Primary School, Alfreton

The Dreaded Rip

As I glared sharply at the dim, flickering light, I felt a chill run through my bones, it was a very creepy feeling. *'Noo!'* came a loud scream. I slowly looked around the corner. What I saw was awful, my brother had just ripped his last pair of trousers.

Charlie Russell (11)

Swanwick Primary School, Alfreton

The Bang

As the bright, beaming moon rose from out of nowhere the sound of the clock echoed around the town of Swanwick, followed by numerous amounts of screeching. All of a sudden a cold sensation flooded my veins. A bang came from behind. 'Argh!' I screamed. A black figure me …

Max Parkin (11)
Swanwick Primary School, Alfreton

Arggh!

As I stood in front of the large oak door, my body was shivering all over. The cold night air brushed against my face. I could hear echoes bouncing off the castle walls. Suddenly the castle door creaked open. 'Arggh!' I screamed as my grandma confronted me.

Sam Watson (11)

Swanwick Primary School, Alfreton

Untitled

As the door slowly opened, I stepped in. Inside was an everlasting dark, gloomy hallway. It was deserted but just as I was about to open the living room door, a clown tapped repeatedly on my shoulder.
'Oh, I do hate young children's party entertainers!' I bellowed.

Ashley Poulter (11)
Swanwick Primary School, Alfreton

The Shock

I had just got back from my granny's. I was so tired that I went to bed. Just as I lay down I heard an ear-piercing scream! I quickly ran down the stairs, round the corner was my brother crying because he'd just been beaten on his Xbox 360.

Eddie Stevenson (10)

Swanwick Primary School, Alfreton

The Halloween Fright

She saw a trail of dark red blood. Then suddenly
without warning she heard a scream. She ran as
fast as she could, yanked the door open.
'What're you doing here?' her friend said.
'You were screaming and there's blood
everywhere.'
She replied, 'I'm just rehearsing the Halloween
Play.

Sarah Wells (11)
Swanwick Primary School, Alfreton

Toes

Soon as I got home from school I ran into the
bathroom. I heard an ear-piercing scream. As
I opened the door I saw my brother hopping
around with a bright red toe.
'Ha ha!'; I said full of joy. That will teach him to
wear his slippers.

Molly Rice (10)
Swanwick Primary School, Alfreton

268

Alone!

I don't like being alone but since it was my
parent's anniversary I didn't mind. I thought I
heard the door open, then the lights started
flickering, I went to investigate. I heard a voice
behind me.
'Your parents told me to just come in,' it was my
local electrician.

Bradley Meakin (11)
Swanwick Primary School, Alfreton

The Spot Horror

After a miserable day at school, Emily stalked off into her bedroom. Listening to her iPod, a terrifying scream slid under the door. *'Argh!'* screamed Jodie. Now Jodie was fourteen, one tiny spot had appeared on the side of her nose. Jodie peered at herself in horror.

Remi Long (10)

Swanwick Primary School, Alfreton

Button Eyes!

It was 11pm. Grace couldn't sleep after watching a scary movie, so she decided to go to her mum. She woke her mum up and she seemed fine until Grace put the light on. With horror she found her with button eyes and blood dripping. What had happened?

Charlotte Burton (11)
Swanwick Primary School, Alfreton

Manchester United

Man U Vs Liverpool. I was so excited and Megan
and Miss Brandwood made a bet. Kick off took
place. I checked the score. 1-0 to Man U. I leapt
around the room. Liverpool scored 1-1. Then
Man U scored again. Man U won, so I'm happy.

Hannah Cory (11)
The Downs CE Primary School, Deal

Boo!

It was afternoon, but McDonald's was already busy. Claire was doing her Saturday afternoon job, (which was to take out the rubbish) when she heard a strange eerie noise coming from one of the dustbins. Anxiously she opened the bin, suddenly her brother jumped out and shouted with excitement, 'Boo!'

Robyn Manning (11)
The Downs CE Primary School, Deal

The Secret Trap

Once upon a time lived a small, chubby boy who always explored the commodious world. One day he found a crumbling and menacing house. He slowly opened the rusty, wooden door and cautiously explored the dusty house. He got stuck in a secret trap, eventually his mum rescued him.

Charlie Drane (10)

The Downs CE Primary School, Deal

The Sausage

One day Sophie and I went swimming to Tides
for Dip 'n' Dine, for lunch. We had sausage and
chips. But Sophie dropped her sausage on the
floor, so Sophie had no sausage and I had to buy
her one, which wasted my money. So much for
the dine part.

Lillie Elle Wadhams (10)
The Downs CE Primary School, Deal

The Scary Door

It was that day when the two boys slowly walked up to the broken door. Nervously they opened it. All they found was an old broken chair. One of the boys sat on it, they then realised there was nothing to be afraid of. They went home laughing.

Max McDonald (10)
The Downs CE Primary School, Deal

Surprise

On my way home it was eerily quiet. The house
stood dark and still. I opened my creaky front
door and heard a dog bark. It shook me up. It was
so dark, then all of a sudden, *click!*
Surprise!' My family held a surprise party. What a
great birthday.

Jack Weale (11)
The Downs CE Primary School, Deal

The Caverns Of Mysterious Events!

Suddenly he ducked! A missile fired straight at him as a gust of strong wind blew. He ran to an entrance, it led to a dull, gloomy cave. Before him was a strange looking man with three eyes and an extraordinarily extensive nose. *Boom!* Immediately he quickly grabbed him.

India Leitner (11)

The Downs CE Primary School, Deal

Holiday Joke Or Not!

My dad has been telling my sister and me that we are going on holiday to New York. While we are there we are going to see the Statue of Liberty, Ground Zero and the Empire State Building. We fly out on 1st April which is April Fools Day!

Megan Maslak (11)
The Downs CE Primary School, Deal

Restaurant Lovers

He took her hand and led her to a little room
beside the restaurant. They sat and talked for a
while. Finally he got down on one knee and said,
'Please marry me!'
Oh wow! She thought, *this is it.*
The couple married and grew old together with
their children.

Katy Gooch (11)
The Downs CE Primary School, Deal

The Crazy Man

In an ancient house, lived a scruffy old man who was so crazy that he was willing to do anything. One day, when the golden sun was shining, the man jumped off an extremely high cliff and died.

Kiean Nelson (10)
The Downs CE Primary School, Deal

My Day Out

One day me, Dana, Sophie, Lillie and Sky all went to Tids. We had lots of fun. We stayed in the pool for three hours. We then went and had some lunch. After that we went and got dressed, then went home.

Chelsea Frost (10)
The Downs CE Primary School, Deal

As I Looked Out

As I looked out of my kitchen window, I saw a squirrel running quickly along the garden fence, and a robin in a tree chirping a merry tune. The washing on the line was flapping in the wind like the sails of a tall sailing ship. *I'm home at last.*

Katie Neary (11)
The Downs CE Primary School, Deal

283

Bedtime

'Bedtime!' called Mum as the clock struck nine.
'OK,' Tom yelled as he trudged up the stairs. Tom
got into bed as quickly as he could, he wanted
to have that dream again. Tom's head smashed
into the soft pillow. His eyes slowly closed as he
wandered off to sleep.

Joshua Cooper (10)
The Downs CE Primary School, Deal

The Dream Of Fantasy

Afilia's head touched the feathery pillow, she fell straight asleep. Her mind got working imagining creatures. In her dream she rode a unicorn. She was having a ball until she met Shrek who chased her. She then woke up in bed. Her eyes opened, Shrek was standing there. She screamed …

Robyn Leech (11)
The Downs CE Primary School, Deal

The Football Gang!

Once there was a football player called Sam. He played for Deal Town Rangers, scored, 40 mins later it was half-time. Second half, Deal Town scored again. The final score was 2-0. Bettshanger lost but they had another game up for grabs against Deal again. They were gonna win.

Tristan Martin (10)

The Downs CE Primary School, Deal

The Never-Ending Nightmare

Ruby squirmed and wiggled. She was in bed
having a loathsome dream. A smelly vile man
gazed down at her. His breath was stale and his
eyes were a piercing green. His jet-black hair was
greasy and needed washing. Suddenly Ruby woke
up; the man was standing over her!

Malindi Parker (11)
The Downs CE Primary School, Deal

287

The Drowned Man

One marvellous summer day an 11-year-old girl called Jodie strolled along the seaside. She heard a noise, it was coming from the sea. It was a man about 20 on boat called Polar Bear, shouting for help. After five minutes of waiting the lifeboat came, he was rescued.

Eloise Inett (10)

The Downs CE Primary School, Deal

The Horrible Nightmare

It was the middle of the night and all around the castle there were owls and foxes. Just then there was a break-in at the palace, a mysterious man got into the princess' room and stole the crown. She could no longer be Queen Aurora.

Bethany Miller (11)
The Downs CE Primary School, Deal

Dumpty Got Boiled

Humpty-Dumpty made a splash as he got dropped into a pot of boiling water. *Tick tock ring!* went the cooking timer. Humpty-Dumpty was fished out with a spoon. He was placed in an egg cup and got his head cut off with a spoon. Too bad, he's gone.

Jack Traviss (10)

The Downs CE Primary School, Deal

The Door Of Darkness

I walked in my room, it was pitch-black and the door slammed shut so I ran into my wardrobe. It wasn't a wardrobe, it was another world and it was pitch-black. 'Ahh!' One light turned on and there was a loud rumble. I ran back to my door.

Olivia Morrison (9)

The Downs CE Primary School, Deal

The Dream I Didn't Want To End

It was night, Mum told me to go to bed because it was a school night. So I stomped upstairs, fell asleep and had a dream. It was a wonderful dream. There were as many sweets as you could ever eat. Just then Mum woke me up. 'School,' she said.

Jessica Wing (10)

The Downs CE Primary School, Deal

My Cave Journey

I was walking along the beach when I saw a hole in the cliff. So I decided to explore it. The cave was extremely dark: but luckily I had my flashlight. I got deeper and deeper into this pitch-black cave when suddenly my torch's batteries ran out. *I'm lost* …

Toby Roberts (11)
The Downs CE Primary School, Deal

My Environment

Birds chirping, the trees dancing, leaves swiftly
laying, next-door's dog howling across the
street. Cats purring to the wind. The trampoline
squeaking once again. My brother squealing
with excitement, the sound of packets of crisps
opening. The smell of freshly cut grass. *Ahh!* To be
home at last. *Lovely!*

Freya Emmerson (11)
The Downs CE Primary School, Deal

Spaceship Mystery

One morning I woke up and I was idly staring out of the window, when a massive spaceship, shaped like a banana, appeared in my front garden! I wanted to investigate so I slung on my clothes and ran into my parents' room to tell them what I'd seen ...

Finley Humphries (10)
The Downs CE Primary School, Deal

Alien In My Garden

One day I opened my bedroom window to see an alien in the garden. The alien was small, green with twenty bulging eyes! I tried to have a conversation with it, but I only got a grunt in reply. The alien loved to eat grass, until one day it disappeared.

Rylan Batley-Thomsett (10)
The Downs CE Primary School, Deal

Untitled

I was dreaming one day that I was a mascot for Tottenham Hotspur. We were getting ready to walk down the tunnel. Luka Modric stood next to me. It was immensely petrifying walking out onto the pitch in front of 35,936. Wow! I wasn't dreaming, it was a reality!

William Orchard (11)

The Downs CE Primary School, Deal

The Never-Ending Nightmare

Amira was running through the woods being chased by a man with many axes in his hand. She ran and ran then suddenly she woke up and rolled over and caught her arm on the axe. She screamed and saw a dark gloomy shadow in the hallway. It was coming.

Kerys Squire (11)
The Downs CE Primary School, Deal

The End Of Time

Dave was sitting in his room thinking about the weekend. When the weekend came a UFO was hurtling towards the Earth. When the ship landed on Earth it made a really big bang, there was a huge pad on the ship so Dave pushed the button and time stopped.

Thomas Slater (11)

The Downs CE Primary School, Deal

Plane Terror

The captain and passengers, obviously terrified, were screaming as loud as they could. They were going to have to crash into a building because the engines weren't working! The captain tried everything he could to regain control of the aeroplane. An eerie voice suddenly boomed: 'Simulation ended!'

Luke Rowland (11)
Whitehills Primary School, Northampton

The Water Adventure

Edward stared at the water, goggles steaming up with excitement. Was this the day he was going to swim? He slowly put one foot, then his whole body, into the water. Then he heard his mother call, 'Don't forget to wash behind your ears honey.' He was in the bath.

Daniel Heap (11)
Whitehills Primary School, Northampton

Darkness

As the clock struck midnight eerie sounds began creeping through me. Ghostly voices echoed, it was darkness! Cold wind filled the room like a blanket covering you. It began getting darker, the room began to get smaller… I woke to find that it was just all a silly imaginary dream.

Chloe Axtell (11)

Whitehills Primary School, Northampton

Feast!

Slowly Svec and Rosalie pulled back the decrepit door; dust arose, shrouded their faces with a ghostly pallor. Two white masks bobbed up from the darkness, gracefully. 'Is it dinner time already?' Robert's perfect teeth gleamed. As the clock struck midnight, the stench of blood hung in the air, harshly.

Nicole Hand (11)

Whitehills Primary School, Northampton

It Comes - It's Over!

Silently, it crept up behind him, gnashing its teeth
as if sharpening them. As Jack opened the gate to
the ominous graveyard, walking in, it pounced.
Jack was stunned so it easily penetrated his
defences. Blood trickled down its straining jaws
as it slumped down after its easy dinner.

Jordanne Suter (10)

Whitehills Primary School, Northampton

Lucky

A dog called Lucky was walking down the road
when he lost his owner. He wandered back
down the road and fell into a ditch. Suddenly a
shadow bent over his body. It was a child! The
dog realised that he was being taken to his owner.
Happy days!

Emily Taylor (10)
Whitehills Primary School, Northampton

Jack Cat

One day, when Mum had taken Tierney and Kye to school, Jack cat decided to have an adventure. He climbed out the window, chased Sid the squirrel, and Beryl and Marg the blue tits, till he was worn out! He slid back in, just as Mum walked through the door.

Tierney Johnson-Springham (8)
Woodlands School, Brentwood

306

The Climbing Wall

One day I went to this park and there was a
climbing wall. I went on it and one foot slipped,
but I pulled myself up! The first time I didn't make
it! The second time halfway! The third time I
made it! *Ding!* 'Hooray!' they all cheered.

Nathan Spenceley (7)
Woodlands School, Brentwood

Untitled

The night sky was clear, with one bright star twinkling. A magic fairy sneezed over me and I flew right into the star. I saw Captain Hook. I saw lots of fairies, I saw clouds. One fairy's name was Tink. I flew up into the air with her.

Lewis Cotier (7)

Woodlands School, Brentwood

What A Surprise!

Georgia could not understand why her pony,
Poppet, was being so grumpy. When ridden
she refused to go any faster than walk, it was
a mystery. After brushing her down Georgia
took her dog for a walk. When she returned
the mystery was solved! Beside Poppet was her
newborn foal.

Georgia Davis (8)
Woodlands School, Brentwood

The Wrong Surprise

One day a little girl was going to somebody's birthday party. It was a surprise party, so when she got there she thought she was the first to arrive, but she wasn't. The birthday girl wasn't there yet. Everybody was already there and they all surprised the wrong girl!

Ivy Samuel (7)

Woodlands School, Brentwood

Coming Home

Olivia gazed out of the car into the rain, looking for a rainbow. Staying with Aunty Theresa was nice, now she was coming home. She leapt from the car and ran into the house, pushing past Daddy and into the lounge. There lay her new baby sister, Grace, sleeping peacefully.

Olivia Shepherd (8)
Woodlands School, Brentwood

The Race

Ben was at the start line for the race. He was nervous and could feel his heart pounding, waiting for the start gun to go off. *Bang!* They were off, running as fast as they could go, the finish was in sight. So nearly, nearly there, hooray! He had won!

Max Watts (7)

Woodlands School, Brentwood

The Shiny Crystal

Maggie was in a cave digging for shiny things. She found a crystal. She thought it was worthless. When Maggie got home she threw it away. The next morning she looked out the window, saw the biggest most beautiful rainbow in the world. Seems the crystal wasn't worthless after all.

Maximus Era (7)
Woodlands School, Brentwood

A Twist In Monkey's Tail

There was once a monkey who was called Minny. Minny always forgot things. He went to his grandfather. Minny told his grandfather that he always forgot things. Grandfather said Minny should put a twist in his tail. Ever since he hasn't forgotten anything, because Minny looks at his tail.

Johanna Zenner (8)
Woodlands School, Brentwood

Walk In The Garden

Nan was walking in the garden, it was a sunny day in March. She heard a rustling in the bushes in front of her, she was scared. Suddenly something came towards her. It was very large, black and hairy. Nan screamed. *Phew!* It was only Kuma Chan, the super dog.

Lily-Rose McDonald (8)
Woodlands School, Brentwood

The Misunderstanding

On his birthday Ethan got a telescope. He set the telescope up in the attic. One night Ethan thought he saw a meteor through his telescope. He got really excited. He called his parents. However it was not a meteor, it was the BA502 from Heathrow - an aeroplane!

Ethan Taylor (8)
Woodlands School, Brentwood

The Final Countdown

The ice was cold and there were thirty seconds
on the clock. The noise from the crowd was
deafening. One all, the scoreboard illuminated
in red neon. The puck slid across the smooth
surface. With all my strength my shot flew
through the air and into the goal.

James Newman (9)
Woodlands School, Brentwood

The Picnic

Ben was walking home from school. It was a sunny day. When he arrived home he could hear some noises coming from the garden. All his family were playing bulldog. Ben joined in, they had lots of fun. Ben's mum said, 'Picnic time.' They had cucumber sandwiches and crisps. Yum!

Jack Nevill (9)
Woodlands School, Brentwood

The Beginning Of A Holiday Adventure

Australia at the beach, Mum, Dad, Peter and
Fiona were having a wonderful time. Fiona had
entered into a volley ball game at 15 00. Peter
had entered into a surf competition at 13 00.
Mum and Dad were just sunbathing, reading
magazines and eating ice creams. Their holiday
had truly begun.

Zoe Mallottides (10)
Woodlands School, Brentwood

The Chocolate Covered Beast

One day Joseph turned up at school and had a talk with the caretaker. 'There is a beast roaming about,' he said. Whilst Joseph was on the field he looked out for the monster. He hard a rustling in the grass. It was him, my chocolate-covered, scary-looking headmaster.

William Sullivan (10)

Woodlands School, Brentwood

Seaside Holiday

Today was sunny. We decided to go to the beach.
We packed a picnic, towels and a lilo. People
were arriving and laying out their towels. We ran
into the sea and jumped onto our lilos. Suddenly
there was a bang and it began to rain. The day
was over.

Dalton Pearce (10)
Woodlands School, Brentwood

Saga

Last night a Boeing 747 almost crashed. The plane
took off from Heathrow heading for Florida. The
plane had 185 people on board. Halfway through
the flight a flock of birds flew into the engines.
The pilots lost control over the Atlantic, but they
landed safely and became heroes.

Bradleigh Power (10)

Woodlands School, Brentwood

A Holiday Adventure At The Beach

Holidays! After breakfast I went downstairs to the beach where I saw dolphins hovering gracefully in the water. I stepped towards one. It did not swim away! I got on its back. Suddenly I was flung into the sea. I was far away from the shore but I swam back.

Katharina Zenner (11)
Woodlands School, Brentwood

Pixie Path

It was early one morning. I got out of bed and I had a tingling feeling on my back. The wings were growing fast. I tried to hide them from Mum but they ripped through my T-shirt and I started to fly. Oh what *joy!*

Bernice Rayner (11)
Woodlands School, Brentwood

Sigurd And The Dragon

Sigurd held the sword in front of his face, within a few steps he would be in the cave of the dragon. But as he reached the cave, he saw the dragon dead on the floor. As he looked up he saw another hero flying off with a bloody sword.

Sabrina Singh (10)
Woodlands School, Brentwood

Guinea Pigs Hate Baths

Oh no! She's going to give me a bath! I hate baths. I like the way I smell! I'm in the water and all soapy. I'll make a dash for the draining board. Now it's all over and wrapped in a towel. Safe and cosy with a biscuit to nibble.

Sophie Tucker (11)
Woodlands School, Brentwood

A Dopey Policeman

A woman was walking on the street when she saw a policeman patrolling it. He approached her gradually. She was afraid of being questioned. She could not run away from him. He looked at her and asked, 'Could you tell me where the police station is?' What a dopey man.

Jay Yagnik (11)
Woodlands School, Brentwood

327

Toadstool Temple

We were leaving for holiday, when we ran out of petrol. I got out the car and looked for help, but then I fell in a hole. There were toadstools everywhere and right in the middle there were toadstools that looked like temples. I was dreaming.

Amelia Bright (10)

Woodlands School, Brentwood

Information

We hope you have enjoyed reading this book - and that you will continue to enjoy it in the coming years.

If you like reading and writing, drop us a line or give us a call and we'll send you a free information pack. Alternatively visit our website at www.youngwriters.co.uk

Write to:
Young Writers Information,
Remus House,
Coltsfoot Drive,
Peterborough,
PE2 9JX

Tel: (01733) 890066
Email: youngwriters@forwardpress.co.uk